Praise for Ana Menéndez's

The Last War

"A potent literary novel. . . . A deft portrait of an estranged couple whose pain is veiled by the fog of war." —*People*

"Speaks to Ana Menéndez's maturity—as a woman and a writer. . . . [It] evoke[s] the macabre merry-go-round of reporters who have whirled in and out of Iraq. . . . A character study of those who have found their purpose in bearing witness to bloodshed." —*New York Times Book Review*

"Menéndez shows with unblinking honesty in her self-assured second novel, *The Last War*, how in conflict and its aftermath journalists can find or lose themselves. . . . Menéndez's deep wisdom about people and their relationships is the payoff that always makes this insightful author worth reading."
—*St. Louis Post-Dispatch*

"Menéndez is a skilled novelist—even admirers of her acclaimed short story collection, *In Cuba I Was a German Shepherd*, or her earlier novel, *Loving Che*, will be impressed with the deepening maturity of her writing. . . . A fully convincing psychological portrait."
—*South Florida Sun Sentinel*

THE LAST WAR

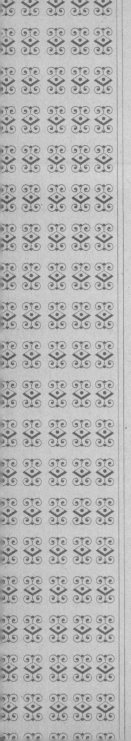

THE
LAST
WAR

A NOVEL

ANA MENÉNDEZ

HARPER ● PERENNIAL

NEW YORK ● LONDON ● TORONTO ● SYDNEY ● NEW DELHI ● AUCKLAND

HARPER ● PERENNIAL

A hardcover edition of this book was published in 2009 by HarperCollins Publishers.

P.S.™ is a trademark of HarperCollins Publishers.

HarperCollins books may be purchased for educational, business, or sales promotional use. For information please write: Special Markets Department, HarperCollins Publishers, 10 East 53rd Street, New York, NY 10022.

FIRST HARPER PERENNIAL EDITION PUBLISHED 2010.

Designed by Susan Yang

The Library of Congress has catalogued the hardcover edition as follows:

Menéndez, Ana.
    The last war : a novel / Ana Menéndez.—1st ed.
        viii, 340 p., [16] p. of plates : col. ill., map ; 24 cm.
    ISBN: 978-0-06-172476-3
    1. Photojournalists—Fiction. 2. War correspondents—Fiction. 3. Americans—Middle East—Fiction.
    4. Married people—Fiction. I. Title.
PS3563.E514 L37 2009
813'.54 22   2008040919

ISBN 978-0-06-172477-0 (pbk.)

10 11 12 13 14 ID/RRD 10 9 8 7 6 5 4 3 2 1

For my niece, Elle

Most journalists are restless voyeurs who see the warts on the world, the imperfections in people and places. Gloom is their game, the spectacle their passion, normality their nemesis.

—GAY TALESE

I don't like being a voyeur, looking into other people's marriages.

—PAUL BEGALA

THE LAST WAR

Chapter 1

In Istanbul that summer the mornings were very still, and I could sometimes hear a boy's faint voice calling out in the dark. I was waking before sunrise from nights that seemed impossibly long, and rather than linger in bed I often took my coffee out to the terrace and sat looking at the lights that shifted and dimmed on the far shore. Whether because of the watery world and the constant lapping of the Bosporus or because of my state of mind at the time, most everything those days seemed tinged with a liquid mutability. The boy's voice, calling through the fog, was the only solid thing, a vessel that gave equal shape to hope and sorrow. Every morning the boy called out his impossible promises, and every morning I guessed at the meaning of the words I couldn't understand: *Fresh greens delivered to your door. Sweet berries for your love. Herbs to ease your pains.*

Two months earlier, my husband had left to cover the war in Iraq. I remained in Istanbul, telling friends I was waiting for my accreditation papers to come through. This wasn't really a lie: though I shot almost exclusively for Brando's paper now, I was still considered a freelancer and, of course, had to arrange everything for myself. But the deeper truth, of which I was only dimly aware, was that something essential had begun to give way in my marriage. And though I could not describe it exactly, I could sense it most at night when, with eyes closed and still caught inside a dream, I understood that the disillusion we had so long been running from had finally come for us.

We were the war junkies: Eros and Chaos, endlessly drawn to the ragged margins where other people hated and died. It was as if we believed constant movement would deliver us finally from the disappointments of an ordinary life. For years, it seemed true enough. He was a writer, I was a photographer, and from war to war, we made a team.

We had met in the run-down suburban bureau of a midsize paper in a midsize town with pretensions of big-city glory. I hated him instantly: he was a pretty boy who, I suspected, slept in his white button-downs from Brooks Brothers. If I caught him looking at me as I made my way to the darkroom, I turned away. If he stepped in front of me, I moved aside. Then one night we rode out to an assignment together—a shooting at a downtown liquor store. On the way back, he told me he'd gone to Cambridge and was going to be a war correspondent. He was not yet thirty years old. I sat next to him in the front, resting a camera on my lap. At a light, he pointed to the almost full moon above us. Then he turned to me and recited the first lines of "Dover Beach." I stared at him until he asked if I knew Matthew Arnold. Not sure, I said—where does he sit? It was the beginning of our private joke. Matthew Arnold: journalist and poet. We decided later that he would have been back in features, brooding and ironic. Or maybe working as a crazed copy editor on the rim, always complaining about not having time for his "writing."

The tide is full, the moon lies fair upon the straits. Brando was still in his striped tie, but the white button-down was wrinkled and damp. "He knew war," Brando said. "And he knew it was neither glorious nor sordid, just us." I watched his face, crisscrossed by streetlamps, as we drove back to the newsroom through the empty streets. There was more to the prepster than I had thought. Something sweetly dangerous, as if violence were really a way to protect the fragile self. There were other men, other loves, but even to the end, even when everything was lost, I never tired of Brando. He was the always fascinating mystery that I was to myself.

At our wedding, he insisted, over my mother's objections, on reciting the poem. Such a gloomy poem for a wedding, my mother said sadly. But I heard in it then only the lilting raw truth of things. *Ah, love, let us be true to one another! For the world, which seems to lie before us like a land of dreams, so various, so beautiful, so new, hath really neither joy, nor love, nor light, nor certitude, nor peace, nor help for pain . . .* Platitudes to the old, perhaps; but shivering revelation to me at twenty-three, and nothing I could ever forget. I was young and sheltered, as ignorant of life as I was of writers and writing. I understand now that the poem shaped me by shaping the world I was only then getting to know. Some kinds of art can do that. And Brando had initiated me. Brando, who was everything my gray and traumatized parents were not.

We had some good years, more than is decent to wish for. We saw the world together, two tough-acting innocents on leave from what they might have been. In Rome, it was cold and we got lost. We stopped in a plaza for directions and bought a bottle of wine and a corkscrew. We arrived at the hotel many hours later, but happy. That night, I washed my sweater in the bathroom sink and hung it out on the balcony railing. There was a full moon, and I lay in bed with my arm around Wonderboy's back as my sweater moved in the breeze and the moon illuminated the balcony, the bed, all the city, and us in it.

In France, he insisted we stop at every provincial square so that I could take a photo of him next to the monument to fallen soldiers. He stood straight and proud next to all that stained history.

The years passed. In Sri Lanka, we lay beneath mosquito netting for the first time and listened to bombs falling in the distance. When I slipped out of bed to shoot from the window, he yelled: It's dangerous! In Kargil, the crashing was a little closer, the road that took us there more perilous. At night, the hotel windows rattled from the concussions. In Kashmir, for the first time, he said the sound of shelling just over the hills sounded beautiful, like summer. In Afghanistan, we traveled together to an execution where young boys ran up and down the bleachers selling fruit juice and cakes. The Talibs handed a shotgun to the victim's brother, who shot wildly and without effect until someone had to come and help him finish what he probably had never meant to start.

So it went after the brief European honeymoon: wars and more wars, mass graves, suicide bombings—our great conjugal tour of all that was wrong and broken in us. Everywhere we went, Wonderboy did all the work, made all the travel arrangements, secured the hotels and the translators, and I came along at the end of it, his shooter. It was always freelance work; the papers he worked for then acted as if they were doing us a favor, allowing their boy wonder to travel with the wife. After a few years, I had a chance to join a paper on the West Coast. The photos from the first Kashmir trip had enjoyed modest praise. But when I broached it with Wonderboy, he stood very still, his hands by his side, the great bulk of him unmovable, as if he were physically blocking me. He said it was up to me. In the end, I turned them down, but the first crack had formed. A few months later we were living in Delhi when India tested its first nuclear bomb. It was the summer of 1998, and the opening thunderclap of our endless war.

Brando Price Phillips. His mother, a film fanatic to the end, had named him after Marlon Brando. Wonderboy hated the name and had a habit of not responding to it until eventually someone called him by something else, usually Phillips or Phil or—a favorite of the jokester newsroom photographers—Phyllis. A few of us took to calling him Wonderboy after an assistant state attorney called the office asking for him and, forgetting his name, referred to him as "that boy wonder you have there, the blond one." And the funny thing is, he did look like a young Brando, handsome, broad-shouldered, manly, and straightforward in an age when such charms were fast going out of fashion. He had a demeanor that invited pet names: serious, but always on the edge of a smile. The prepster look, I came to learn, was an act, a way to hold people at a safe distance. With time, I learned why he met life with a gentle snobbery. For the beautiful, the world is already too close, too familiar, too eager to simulate intimacy. In fact, Wonderboy came from a once-comfortable family. But his parents divorced young, with two small children, and Brando grew up in the Florida Panhandle, where his mother managed a small hotel. He paid his own way to Cambridge, where he picked up the uniform of white button-downs and rep tie that he would wear for the rest of his life.

Chapter 2

We moved to Istanbul just before the first anniversary of September 11. Most Americans may not have realized that war with Iraq was inevitable by then, but we did. Spend enough time around men who think day and night of nothing but fighting, and you get to know what they mean when they open their mouths to talk peace and security.

We had argued about the war, like everyone else. I thought invasion was a bad idea, Wonderboy thought it brilliant. He believed Colin Powell; I didn't. Not that our little disagreements made any difference to the greater story. Peace is a nice idea, Brando had taught me, but the human being is primed for violence. *The warrior will always triumph over the poet, and everything else is fairy tale.*

Of course, the war did nothing to change the way we lived. When you're an American abroad, suffering is for the locals. Our new apartment overlooked the Dolmabaçe mosque, rising in a little neighborhood called Gümüşsuyu. It was a four-bedroom flat with a view that took in all of the Bosporus from Ortaköy to the Marmara Sea. On clear days, the Princess Islands appeared in the distance. Once a month, the full moon rose over the Asian hills, and the city shone beneath it, enchanted.

It was one of the perks of being a foreign correspondent—being allowed to live several social classes above one's means while the paper paid for everything, like some kind of aloof rich uncle. The Istanbul apartment, like the others we had lived in during our decade abroad, was an inheritance of sorts: a luxury hand-me-down from the previous bureau chief. With it came a downtown office, a black Mercedes, and a staff that included Erkan, the driver; Alif, the office manager; and Fatma Gül, Madam Rose, who came every weekday to do the cleaning.

Earlier that winter, Erkan had driven us to dinner and to a few parties, and Wonderboy had held my hand in the backseat. We knew it wasn't forever, and that made it sweet. After Brando left, car and driver were mine alone, and I set upon the city with an enthusiasm that now seems misplaced, almost hysterical. Glassware at Paşabahçe, curtains by the old aqueduct, expensive furniture from Maçka. And so those first days on my own, Istanbul went by in bright, brief frames; the Mercedes gliding past shop windows crowded with radios and cell phones, open-air restaurants with revolving slabs of meat, men waiting for the commuter vans, couples walking arm in arm, men selling fruit from wooden carts, old gypsy women sitting next to cloths draped with silver bangles and earrings, lines in front of the *simit* carts. And then on through the plumbing district, with pipes arranged on outdoor tables; the flower district, with the red and pink roses; the light district, where every window blazed.

Here and there a demonstration, young men holding signs that I couldn't read, shouting things I couldn't hear from the cool interior of the car that kept moving—hermetic and sterile—across the bridge and into Asia, where the women dressed modestly, and household goods were reasonably priced. Then back again, the bridge stopped with traffic, and me alone in the back, suspended over the Bosporus, the shimmering water, the white gulls that swooped and dove over the domes of the mosques, the needle minarets.

When Brando entered Iraq in the spring of 2003, driving himself through the desert, I was on the road between Bebek and the old fort, being driven around the imperial city like the favored concubine in an old story.

Chapter 3

I furnished the apartment, hung a few paintings, and bought a new rug, a ritual of ours in each new home. When there was nothing left to do, I kept busy with a few assignments. A food magazine sent a reporter to do a piece on Ottoman cuisine—it had been planned long before the war—and hired me to shoot some of the sights. A freelancer based in Moscow came to do a story on honor killings and hired me to illustrate it. It was for pennies, but it got me out of Istanbul for a few days. Diyarbakir was near the Iraq border, but you wouldn't know a war was going on across the frontier. People went about their daily work, like everywhere else. I shot the sad and dusty village where a girl had been murdered by her brother and then flew back to the city, splurging on a business-class seat. I returned to the apartment very late. Madam Rose had left the curtains open, and the first sight of the illuminated city beyond the glass made me pause in gratitude.

In between assignments, I roamed the city, making a visual diary of Istanbul that might outlast my stay there.

The first time I walked into the Hagia Sophia, I stood quietly, without the camera, waiting for my eyes to adjust. The former church was perpetually under renovation, and the great dome remained obscured behind layers of scaffolding. Still, you could walk slowly, staring at a fixed point, and succumb to the illusion that the heavens tilted gently away from you. The renovation was a kind of hopeful madness: everyone knew the church would not survive the next big quake. Already some of the pillars were bending, the whole shifting dome one last crisis from vanishing forever. Upstairs, a guide explained a new earthquake detection system to a group of middle-aged men and women. They stood on the tips of their Teva sandals and shook their heads with the forced piety of strangers on a package tour.

For two weeks, I traveled the tourist places one by one. I took my shoes off at the Blue Mosque and sat in the back to copy the tile patterns into my notebook; I lit candles at San Antuan of the floating Christ; I rode the trolley at sunset. I took a ferry up the Bosporus to a village at the mouth of the Black Sea and shuddered at the way the water seemed to drop off beyond the narrows, certain I had come suddenly to the world's deep, blank edge.

One hot day I descended into the Sunken Palace and discovered the two Medusas floating just above the water, their eyes open wide in some horror that had chased them down a thousand years. I shot them. The long exposure rendered them glowing and a little blurry in the green underwater light.

Chapter 4

Brando called from the war, sometimes even twice a day. The satellite phone muffled his voice so he always sounded sick. But those first few weeks after the invasion, the connections were good, and it was easy to believe his upbeat reports.

The paper had rented a mansion on the Tigris, just outside the green zone. Workers had already renovated the outside deck and resurfaced the swimming pool. Now a truck came around every afternoon to fill the pool with ice. In the evenings, while the others swam, Wonderboy went for a run along the river.

"It's an exciting time to be here," he said, his nasal voice bouncing off some orbiting metal in space and back again to me. "You can feel the historic plates shifting."

Each time, I promised it would be only a few days before I could join him. And then the next day, I delayed some more. In my defense, I had already made an inventory of the equipment I needed—the digital revolution had vastly simplified war photography. And I had long since ordered away for another Vivitar 285, worried about the constant rumors that my favorite flash was about to be discontinued. British Airways had not resumed their promised flights to Baghdad, but a Lebanese outfit had started a charter service, and there was talk that Royal Jordanian might soon offer one also. I wasn't avoiding Baghdad. At least, I didn't think I was. But early in May, when I got an assignment from a Japanese magazine to shoot Ottoman tombs, I accepted immediately. It was for a good amount of money, plus expenses, and I could not pass it up. Besides, the subject intrigued me. When I mentioned it to Wonderboy, there was a long pause at the other end. I was missing the war, he said finally. Why did I want to hang around Istanbul anyway?

"I'm working," I said. "Same as you."

"Anything wrong?"

Something else had come into his voice, and I couldn't explain what it was. Suspicion?

"What could be wrong? I got an assignment. They're paying $8,000 U.S. We'd be stupid to turn it down."

Chapter 5

The first place on the list was the royal crypts near the Blue Mosque, and one early Monday morning when the light was good and clear, I drove out there with Erkan. But as soon as he pulled away to park, I knew it would be a wasted trip. The building was squat and ugly, utterly out of place amid the soaring monuments of the old city. Inside, it was no better. A single lonely guard nodded to me as I slipped off my shoes. The crypts looked like miniature pool tables, each covered in green felt; all those glorious lives united in one final equalizing ugliness. I motioned to the guard with my camera, and he bobbed his head yes. But there was nothing worth shooting. A wide-angle might have worked, but there wasn't room enough to maneuver. I walked once around the awkward space. On my second pass I noticed that the light coming through a small high window shone almost perfectly on the plate over one of the crypts. I crouched and took a few shots with the 78mm. I shot out until the light shifted. Then I stood to read the inscription:

Sultan Amurath was so strong he could easily lift 200 kilograms and pull the hardest bowstrings. The arrows he fired could even pierce shields, while his spears flew great distances.

Another ancient blowhard. There was something oddly comforting in it, the enduring desire for glory. I put my camera away. On the way out, I dropped a coin in the guard's collection can. He said something to me in Turkish and smiled. A cat lounged at his feet, and unable to resist, I stepped back into the sun and shot a few more frames.

On my way out, I brushed shoulders with a woman in a black abaya. I turned quickly to excuse myself, but she had already crossed the sidewalk as if she were in a great hurry. People were always bumping against each other in Istanbul—there was nothing unusual about it. The anxiety that suddenly came over me I attributed to the tombs and the long-dead nobility that continued to passively reign there.

Erkan was waiting for me near the obelisk.

"Very good, yes?" he said.

"Evet," I said in my childlike Turkish. "Çok iyi."

"Harika," he said.

"Harika," I echoed.

By the time you're dealing in third and fourth languages, communication is stripped down to its most essential parts: *Yes. Very good. Wonderful.* I didn't know if this made for purer thought or if after years of resorting to simple expression I was now incapable of any kind of complex reasoning.

✿   ✿   ✿

I arrived at my apartment just as the afternoon call to prayer was ending. Me tired, I thought to myself and laughed. *Yorgunum.* It was Friday, the day the mail usually came from New York, and the FedEx packet was waiting outside the front door.

I poured myself a glass of wine and sat on the couch with the mail. Even though most of it was always for Brando, I loved getting that weekly package. Now and then there would be something for me, a letter from a magazine editor or a check from one of the agencies. The packet that week was heavy, and I knew before opening it that it would be filled with magazines. I tore it open with a knife. Two *New Yorker*s from May and one from April, the *New York Review of Books*, *Harper's*. I don't remember either one of us ever reading any of it, but we continued to get them, as if the bylaws of our caste required it. I flipped through each of the magazines quickly before setting them aside on the couch, where the wind gently rustled them open. American Express, Master-Card, a bank statement from Citibank. I put them each in neat piles, weighing them down with books to protect them from the breeze. Later, I would move them to Brando's desk, where I had arranged his correspondence by category: bills, magazines, letters. Amid all of it, there were only two pieces of mail for me: one that looked like junk ("Open immediately") and another that was addressed to me by hand with my married name (which I had never taken) in parentheses.

It was one of those thin airmail envelopes, and it opened

easily. The letter, just a page long, was typed on onionskin paper, the almost translucent kind my grandparents had once kept in their nightstand.

The page made an elegant sound as I unfolded it. How sumptuous it sounded that first time, and how benign. I read the letter straight through quickly, and then I read it again in parts, hoping to find in the fragments the logic that eluded the whole.

I kept the letter secret for many months. As there is no longer any reason to hide it, I reproduce it in its entirety.

Dearest Flash:

Amazing this snail mail! I'd almost forgotten how.

I don't have your e-mail—somewhere in my travels I lost it, and the foreign desk wouldn't give it to me. Obviously I didn't want to send anything to Brando. They suggested a letter, so here it is!

So, first, congratulations on the move. Are you happy? Saw your name on a Web site for "artists of color." You must be so proud!

I'm back in Amman, the days are lovely, especially after Baghdad. No complaints, though. I'll finally get to finish that photo essay on Arab women, and it was good to be on the road again, shooting to my heart's content. But what a bear Iraq is—and now with that translator getting killed. Chills.

That's one reason I wanted to get in touch, to find out how you are holding up under the strain. I feel so bad for you. I can't believe your husband has done it again. Is doing it again. Why can't the asshole keep his pants zipped? (Sorry, but that's how I feel. Sorry.) I met the young woman, Nadia or whatever her name is, pretty girl. She's always around the house, and John thinks it's very funny. Manly and all that.

I suppose you know all about it and don't care a fig. Of all the things to build a marriage on, deception is probably as good as any. What I don't understand is why you haven't left him yet. I can't believe you actually love him. All alone there in Istanbul— What do you get out of that life anyway? Is it the security? If so, you have a surprise coming: he's really flopping in Iraq, and the word is he's going to get pulled off pretty soon, or even fired. Maybe he's spending too much time with the lovely Nadia.

I'm sorry to be the one to tell you this, but know that I'm thinking of you and praying that you'll be strong enough to tell your husband what he really is (a xi8!!@!!) and stop being played for a fool when you're not and you have friends who care.

Much love,
Mira

I folded the letter, opened it, folded it. Read it again. Folded it and put it back in the envelope. There was no return address. But the letter had been postmarked in Jordan. The stamp featured a smiling King Hussein.

Who did we know in Jordan? A shooter. But who? The Mira thing was bullshit. I didn't know any Mira. Or was the writer telling me, "Look"?

Flash. Lots of people called me that. Years back, I'd even had a small exhibition in New York under the name Flash More-Gun. Silly stuff you regret later when war stops being a game. But the name stuck. The other photographers in Kashmir had so baptized me for my inexperienced overuse of the 285. They didn't know I'd had one disastrous shoot where, in haste and fear, I'd miscalculated apertures, and every picture was dark soup. After that, I just stuck the flash on everything. The garish shadows became a kind of signature—one of the ways that error, even the banal kind, marks us forever.

Dearest Flash. Dearest Flash. Dearest. Nadia. I knew the name. Brando himself had mentioned her—a coordinator for the World Food Program in Afghanistan. She must have been transferred to Baghdad. "She's very beautiful," Wonderboy had told me, and his voice had been so smooth at the time that the words didn't catch. He'd met her after the invasion, a week after I'd left Kabul to attend a cousin's wedding in Miami. Nadia. From California, somewhere north. Our Afghan translator, Wonderboy told me, had fallen in love with her.

Nadia. Nadia. Nothing. Nada. It was dark out. Night already? I sat for a long time, not moving. I woke in front of the computer, googling Nadia and Afghanistan. Nadia and World Food. Nadia and translator. Within an hour I had learned all about her sweet nature, her selfless devotion, her work on behalf of the poor and dispossessed. What an absolute crock of shit. What a goddamn fool my husband was. This repressed little blonde from her rich little town, displacing her longings all over the map and calling it charity. What was he thinking? How could he destroy our life together, turn his back on everything we had done as a team, for this? But was she really so beautiful?

My hands shook where they held the thin paper. Who wrote it? Who would do this? A woman. And the more I thought of it, the more convinced I became: a woman had written the letter. It had to be a woman, a woman full of unrealized desires and vague notions of romantic love. A man's taste for pain runs to its blunter forms. Men are daylight sadists; women have spent too many generations laboring in silent anonymity and unspoken resentments. For their pleasure, they build trenches in the heart's night.

Sleep and I became two fugitives, chasing each other in the dark. We circled, hid, raced down corridors that narrowed to a pinhole, a memory. And then I woke, the sound of the clock marking time.

A month after we had moved to Istanbul, I returned from an assignment to find an unfamiliar book on a shelf, spine cracked, the title rubbed away. Now I jumped out of bed and went searching for it. Moonlight filled the apartment, setting the white marble to glowing. It was the middle of summer, but night had chilled the rooms. I shivered in my bare feet.

I found it high up on another shelf, in the book cabinet at the front of the receiving room. It was a slim, leather-bound volume. I opened it to the first page. Bashō, *The Narrow Road to the Deep North*. I sat on the floor, in front of the book cabinet, and began to read: *I, too, have long been tempted by the cloud-moving wind, filled with a deep desire to wander.* I read until the dawn call to prayer shook the windows, read looking for clues, to understand not what was written, but everything behind it, to know why Nadia had given this book to my husband and why he had kept it, lovingly worn, in our home all these months.

Nadia. Sweet humanitarian Nadia . . .

Travel long enough, and you learn not to examine your life at three in the morning. Three in the morning is the time for sleep; it is not a time for thinking. It is the mind's private hour, and good sense and propriety deem that she should not be disturbed in her work. All the dregs of the day are called forth at three in the morning, and they should not be glimpsed until they have been plowed under again by dreams and daylight. The ragged edges of consciousness, the things you don't want to know or see, the failures and regrets of a life dimly lived—they are churning in the hours before dawn. Margarita Anastasia Morales, American daughter of a broken Dominican father, only child of divorce, spic, illegal, quiet loser. Flash, the remade sensualist who escaped all that old-country bullshit in exchange for the rest of the world. For whom feeling became an expression on some foreign face, a frame soon to be forgotten or replaced by another of greater joy or suffering. All surface and light. But, ay mami, you don't know how private defeat can be until you have been betrayed like a regular nobody, spent a night crying in the dark for a man who left you long ago.

Chapter 6

The phone began to ring at nine. I didn't check it until the afternoon—seven missed calls. At five Alif called me, her voice rising. "Brando is desperate to reach you," she said. "Are you all right?"

"Yes, of course," I said.

"Are you sure?"

"Of course," I said, and then thought to add, "I had turned off my ringer and forgot."

"Well," she said, her voice growing soft again. "I'll let him know."

I was going to hang up, but couldn't help adding: "Is he OK?"

"Far as I know," she said.

"OK," I said.

"I'll tell him to call you," she said. "OK?"

"OK."

"Ciao, ciao, babe."

I had always liked Alif and her mellow slang, and now it soothed me. She had a no-nonsense manner that she must have picked up in America and now wore like a slightly garish but beloved travel souvenir.

When the phone rang again near seven o'clock, I picked it up.

"Flash, man, where have you been?"

"Sorry, forgot to turn on the ringer."

"Tunes, man, don't do that to me. I have enough to worry about here without you going AWOL."

I was quiet for a moment and then said, "I'm sorry." And then immediately I thought: Why did I say that? Why should I be sorry?

"I was just worried," Brando said, his tone softer now.

"What's that noise?" I asked.

"What noise?"

"That."

"That boom? Those are bombs. Outgoing."

"Where are you calling from?"

"The roof."

"Why, what's the matter with calling from your room?"

"What are you talking about?"

"You used to call from your room."

"The reception's better up here."

Had there been a pause? Yes, there had been a pause. What did it mean? I didn't know. The pause? It meant nothing or everything.

I almost asked him about the letter. But I held back. I wanted to be standing in front of him, wanted to see his face when he answered. I wanted to look into his eyes. And if I had gotten my chance? If I had, one quiet day, the two of us alone, turned to ask him about the letter? Maybe cooked him dinner and then, after cookies and Sauternes, said, Look at this. All calm and mature. He might have answered: My dearest love, how terrible to get this letter, how you must have suffered. . . . But I knew my husband, knew how war had worn him down, worn the both of us down to little nubs of pain and outrage. Wonderboy, the adventurous innocent poised at the edge of his dream, might have grasped my sadness and been moved to comfort me. But Brando the war correspondent would have lashed out, You believe this shit? How dare you believe this shit? Me risking my goddamn life out there, and you hoarding this poison here. How dare you, how dare you doubt me. . . .

It makes no difference anyway. I was never going to leave Wonderboy. I was incapable of it then, and I'm incapable of it now, even when the question has no meaning.

Chapter 7

In the past I had worked through whatever troubles. But now I could not pick up the camera. The obsession for the image was gone. And when obsession goes, so does the work. I understood why so many painters cultivated madness; it kept desire flowing. Depression is not madness, it's just depression, the loser version, the low-energy response to bad stuff that happens in your life. When you're depressed, you think you're the only one to have ever tasted this kind of hurt. And that lonely self-regard brings with it its own painful pleasure. Only a few months into the invasion, and I had already become a *victim*, a casualty of war. And the exquisite sadness gave my little life something I could call meaning.

I spent several days in this state, steeped in the nobility of my suffering. Madam Rose would come by every morning. I would meet her at the landing and then I'd point to my head, as if I had a migraine—which I did suffer from in my twenties—and I'd walk back to my room, close the door, and wait for her to leave.

"Teşekkürler," I'd say.

"Rica ederim," she'd respond. I felt a little guilty over her look of concern.

Erkan tried calling a few times, but I didn't answer. After a few days of this, I called Alif and told her I was sick.

"Let me tell Erkan to take you to the American hospital."

"Thanks, Alif, it's OK."

"Seriously, it's right there in Maçka."

"Really, I'll be fine. Thanks, Alif."

"Your call, babe."

A few minutes later, Wonderboy called. The first thing he did was ask me about my migraine.

"I don't have a migraine."

"Alif said you were sick."

"You talk to Alif?"

"She wrote. She was worried."

"I'm fine, just a little tired."

Brando didn't follow up. Had he always been like this? The summer, he said, was turning out to be smoky and brutal. And now a correspondent from Boston had arrived in Baghdad and was fighting with the staff over the proper way to sear a steak. "Un-fucking-believable."

"How's the work?" I said.

"Lots of boom-boom," he said. "Mostly outgoing, so far."

He didn't ask about the Ottoman tombs project either, took his monologue right into another story about one of his translators whose brother had been killed by Saddam.

"When he went to claim the body, they made him pay for the bullets," Wonderboy said. "Can you believe that?"

It was his way of saying he and Colin had been right about the war all along.

Chapter 8

I hadn't gone shopping since the day of the letter. I was down to a carton of yogurt and some cherry juice. Worse, the wine was gone. I couldn't deal with Erkan or the ridiculous Mercedes. On the fifth morning, I slipped out while Madam Rose was ironing my T-shirts and hailed a cab in front of the bank. "Maçka, MacroCenter." And what was the word for please? I took out my little notebook. "Lütfen."

It was a good system, my little notebook of phrases (the first and most important phrase, whatever the country: "A glass of red wine, please"). Literary types make a big deal about language, but in truth, there are just a few phrases that you need to know to get by. The most important are: "My name is," "Where's the bathroom?" "Some water," "Please," "Thank you," "I'm sorry," "Good morning," "Good night." Anything more complicated just mucks things up. In restaurants you can point at the menu. All you need to be specific about is the drink: "Water, no ice, and a glass of red wine." *Bir bardak kırmızı şarap istiyorum*. It was the first thing I'd learned in Turkish, long before we even moved to Istanbul.

It was the fall of 1999, after the earthquake. Wonderboy and I had stayed for three weeks at the Çirağan, making daily trips to devastated outskirts and returning in time for a good meal and bottle of wine by the water. Istanbul enchanted us at first glance. We knew one day we'd return here to live. *Bir bardak kırmızı şarap*, "I would like a glass of red wine": it was still the longest sentence I could say in almost any language outside my own.

For work, you just needed to add a few more words and phrases: "Be careful," "very dangerous," "gun," "bomb," "I am a photographer." Simple driving directions: "left," "right," "straight." "Here." "Wait." "Quick." Over the years I'd added a few not-so-obvious phrases that worked like magic. Two are worth noting: "I'm so dumb" and "You're so kind." Even in the worst bind, those two could carry you through, more often than not with a good laugh. Everywhere in the world, people want to hear that they're kind. Even the Taliban wanted to be told they were good people.

The only problem with the notebook system, of course, was responses. If you formed a phrase even reasonably well, the native speaker often assumed you could understand the language and returned with rapid-fire sentences that meant nothing. Still, this wasn't as big a problem as it might seem at first. If you remained calm, you could usually figure out what the person was saying by where he pointed and the expression on his face. And if all else failed, you could pull out one of the other Important Words to Know: "Yes," "No," "Maybe," and the all-purpose favorite, no matter where you traveled in the world: "You may be right."

The cabdriver prattled on, and I nodded now and then. "You may be right," I said. "Evet, evet." He smiled and said something incomprehensible. Evidently, we were both happy with the system. After a short while, he stopped in front of the MacroCenter—it was not so far from the apartment—and I paid him a little bit more than what the meter showed.

"Teşekkürler," he said.

"Çok naziksiniz," I replied. And it's true, he was very kind.

The MacroCenter was one of the great Istanbul institutions. A joy to come into, really. Especially after living in Delhi. There were better places to buy produce and fish—Balık Pazarı, for example. And the lettuce and fruit in the Beşiktaş market still smelled of earth and sun. But I was sad, out of sorts, dragging. I had no energy. I couldn't work. An American-style supermarket was just the thing to restore a sense of order and optimism. I could no more deal with the chaos of the open market than I could deal with Erkan's broken English. I needed sterility, fluorescent lighting, cash registers. You walked into the MacroCenter and you sensed that everything was going to be fine, that someone had it all figured out and all you needed to do was give yourself over to their logic.

I pushed my little cart slowly. Coke Lights, sparkling water, cherry juice. Then to the refrigerated case, where I picked up three pink cans of *beyaz peynir*—feta cheese, though why they didn't just call it that was beyond me. Some shrink-wrapped *pastırma*, a carton of eggs. I passed the line of butchers, who waved and smiled. I didn't know enough Turkish to deal with them. I bought a few packets of pre-packaged meat that looked like lamb. I thought that I should come up with a separate notebook for foods, especially if I was going to be in Istanbul for a while. Then again, did it make any difference if I ate lamb or beef?

I wandered the aisles for more than an hour. Cleaning supplies, brooms, soaps, shampoos, cookies, imported chocolates, oranges, strawberries. At one point, I panicked; I had been in there way too long. But then I relaxed. Who was waiting for me, anyway? No one. I could wander as long and as far as I pleased.

When I was in the soap aisle, my cell phone rang. Wonderboy. I let it go to voice mail.

At the bakery, I picked up a packet of chocolate cookies and a loaf of bread. Then I asked the boy to throw in some Turkish delight. The wines were the last stop, right before the registers. I filled the rest of the cart with bottles of Turkish Gamay. It was pretty much undrinkable, but less offensive than the other Turkish wines and much more reasonably priced than the imports. At the rate I drank red wine, it was the only bottle that made sense. As for the thin, acid taste, I'd long since learned that, exposed long enough, one can get used to almost any outrage.

The cashier mumbled something to me and I said, "Teşekkürler." A boy packed my groceries. I handed the lady my credit card, she ran it, and I signed the slip. "Teşekkürler," I said again. Thank you, thank you. Thanks for the wine, the day, the whole city. The boy carried my bags out to the street and hailed a cab. I handed him 3 million lira, thanked him, got in the cab, and told the driver, "Gümüşsuyu," and of course, he didn't understand. "Gümüşsuyu," I repeated. "Stadium." And finally, "I show."

Madam Rose was gone by the time I returned. I was putting the groceries away when my cell phone rang again. Unavailable. I put the lettuce down and answered, but it was a wrong number. I didn't understand the Turkish and hung up. The woman called again and I said, "Özür dilerim, Turkish yok." And hung up.

The phone rang again, and when I answered, it was the same woman, this time in very precise American English: "Is this the NPR office?"

"You have the wrong number," I said. When the phone rang a fourth time, I let it go to voice mail.

Stupid. But the call unnerved me. Coming so soon after that crazy letter. Surely they were unconnected—the cell phone number, like the apartment, was inherited from the last bureau chief. Still. What did it mean? I finished putting the groceries away and poured myself a glass of wine.

That night, I woke in the dark. I lay in bed for a few moments before realizing it was the call to prayer that had startled me awake. When it was over, I couldn't go back to sleep. That woman's voice, asking for NPR.

I got out of bed and walked down the hall to Wonderboy's office. I had given him the room with the best view, a corner office looking over the Bosporus on one side and, past a low building, to the Topkapı on the other. It's not that I didn't deserve the view. But after a few days there, I felt exposed. The room was right next to the front door, and in those first days in Istanbul, there was a constant procession of visitors and workers into the apartment. The back room, the smallest in the apartment, was more appropriate for me. It had just one window, looking out over the ordinary street. It was private, hidden, quiet. I could close the door and no one would bother me, no one would know I was there.

Wonderboy had set up his big desk by the window, with a battered laptop he'd carried on the Afghan trips. He'd moved in a TV and a couch. But otherwise, he hadn't had time to organize his things. Files tumbled off the desk and to the floor. Books were piled in the corners. He hadn't even put up the curtains. I stood now by the door in the moonlight. Soon it would be day. I stood there for a while, not thinking, just feeling the absence of him. Had it always been like this? Had he always been the missing piece? I took a step back to return to my room. But I couldn't face the dark hallway, the chaste bed.

I had not been sleeping well since the letter. My mind had wrinkled onto itself. That weird phone call. Nothing made sense. One moment, you think you own your days, and the next, all the capriciousness and cruelty that you've kept in a box, that you've regarded from a distance, behind a lens, gets inside of you.

I took a step into the office, and without making an actual decision, I opened the desk drawers and began to go through them. I didn't turn on the light. The night and the moonlight made it all seem like a dream. Receipts, hotel keys, notebooks filled with Brando's unintelligible scrawl. A birthday card, unmarked. Who was it for? Old batteries, notepaper from India, a tiny bronze Ganesh, a gift from me. I flipped through the books. At the bottom of a box I found a brochure from the World Food Programme, British spelling. *What is hunger? What causes hunger? Who are the hungry?*

I turned the brochure around, looking for a phone number, a note. But it was just a brochure on shiny paper, filled with photos of sad, dark-eyed people. I gathered it in one hand and crumpled it.

Morning was beginning to light the Bosporus. I sat at Wonderboy's desk. His laptop sat atop a pile of papers. I looked at it and looked away. I looked at it again. I took it in my hands and turned it around. I set it in front of me and, after a moment, flipped it open and pressed the on switch. Both of us used Eudora, the quirky pre-Outlook system that, like a gossipy friend, never forgot your private correspondence. Even if you were diligent about erasing, all your messages—sent, received, or deleted—were stored on the hard drive, where anyone could access them anytime. The kind of perfect recall that proves the inferiority of machines.

The old Thinkpads took forever to boot up, and it was full morning by the time I opened Wonderboy's account.

There were notes from editors, friends, colleagues. Dull stuff, mostly. "Backread your story." "Barber skedded for 1A." I scrolled quickly through the messages, feeling more and more embarrassed for myself and wondering at the empty days that found me now snooping like a 1950s housewife zonked on Valium and boredom and nearly wishing—could it be?—for something more interesting than the usual infidelity, hoping to learn her husband is not another unimaginative drone screwing his secretary/fixer/colleague but a spy, a misguided patriot, a CIA operative deeply invested in someone else's lie, some other idiocy that would take down a country maybe, but not the dream of us, not the fool hope of two people who knew so little about love that, like trusting children, they opened the door and let the whole bad world in.

From: Nadia <nadia_wfp@yahoo.com>
Date: Sun, 18 Nov 2001 03:00:30—0700 (PDT)
Subject: Re:
Oops sorry—yo you rock but I got the money cause I did not want to pain you—I heard it is a pain getting $ across the border—thank you for helping me—I am excited to get out of here!! You get in on Tuesday night? Let me know what I can do to help you be prepared for a busy week—love, nadia

From: Nadia <nadia_wfp@yahoo.com>
Date: Tues, 20 Nov 2001 15:23:45—0700 (PDT)
Subject: Re:
We could say you are on my board of directors to get

on—info below—just don't use work e-mails—flights
go everyday—better than the drive—I won't do this
for other journos—only you- >> but since you
advise me!!>>
Smiles, nadia

From: Nadia <nadia_wfp@yahoo.com>
Date: Thurs, 29 Nov 2001 22:47:49—0700 (PDT)
Subject: Re:
Thanks dude. I am okay and leaving on the 16th—
ah . . . yesterday was so hard—I saw twins who
stepped on cluster bombs then spent the day with
man (Hazara) who had been tortured by taliban and
said that when he got out he went home and there
was nothing left. his family died when their home
was destroyed in the war—not sure if true cause he
had so much trauma but he was in so much pain.
I am going to put together a welcome to Kabul
packet—I have been so focused on my work I have
not been able to really think too much about other
good stories—but still have some ideas—I'll e-mail
it to you—was gonna leave something at the house
for you but you'll be in later—
Kisses

From: Nadia <nadia_wfp@yahoo.com>
Date: Sat, 15 Dec 2001 03:12:29—0700 (PDT)
Subject: Re:
Okay. But if you want to do any stories on civs he

can find you some extreme cases—like the bus in-
cident yesterday or the case in a village in the south
where 7 people died in one home and the man of the
house was too poor to have their bodies removed—
and then a few k's down the road a man had lost 17
people—no journalists or aid workers have visited.
Let me know the types of angles for things you may
need. I'll write more on that later—You rock dude.
Thanks but for now I am okay. Love, n

My heart beat very fast as I scrolled through the messages. I highlighted them one by one, read them again. Now what? I stared at the screen, the words lit up like a Christmas tree. *Nadia. You rock. Love.*

I shut the computer. What did any of it prove? Since you advise me? Was that code? Maybe they were just friendly letters. They could be read more than one way.

I went back to our room and lay alone in our bed. I lay awake a long time, remembering what it had been like for us. How I used to laugh with Wonderboy in the mornings when he'd swat at the alarm clock, groaning, "Five more minutes . . ."

I had fallen in love fast and hard. In the beginning, Brando would bring me coffee in bed and kiss me lightly on the cheek. Later, those first days would take on a different color, the tender graces overlaid with cold remove, all those chaste kisses prefiguring the many nights I would sleep alone. But it's always happy in the beginning—the great truism of love and revolution. Even when we know nothing good will come of it, we can't keep ourselves from falling.

One night, we threw a dinner party for our friends. It was the sort of meal you make in your twenties: too many bowls and plates and pans and silverware. The first course was ravioli with sage-butter sauce. The main course was chicken and prosciutto skewers. We roasted peppers, cooked rice in the Hitachi, and constructed other side dishes that I can no longer recall. Dessert, I believe, was a cheese flan, a recipe of my grandmother's. We drank several bottles of wine, and the last guest, a notorious overstayer of welcomes, didn't leave until it was past three in the morning. I was so tired. The kitchen, un-air-conditioned in the middle of that summer, was piled with dishes. We didn't have a dishwasher, and Wonderboy must have seen me pause at the door. Go to sleep, he said, we'll do them together in the morning.

I slid fast into dreams and don't remember when he joined me in bed. The next morning I woke beside him. He had a beautiful back and strong, wide shoulders from his rowing years at Cambridge. When I opened my eyes again, it was the middle of the afternoon. Bliss vanished when I remembered the dishes. I left him sleeping and wandered into the kitchen to find that every dish had been washed, every pot scrubbed and put away. The counters gleamed.

He wasn't like the Latin boys I had known, wasn't my father leaning back in his chair after a meal. Loving Brando would be neither escape nor rejection—it would be something much bigger, something momentous and strange. And the fact that I didn't know what it was made me want it all the more.

Chapter 9

I remember little of the days that followed the letter. A succession of sameness. Walks to nowhere. Sights that meant nothing to me. Indecipherable plaques on obscure buildings. Other people's history. What was I doing here? Without my noticing it, Istanbul had abandoned me. Suddenly, it began shifting too easily with the mood of light, going from yellow to gray in minutes, betraying the sense of the eternal that had first seduced me. I walked and walked and the city receded before me: palaces and cemeteries, empty monuments, devastation. It was a glorious summer, the days warm. But the narrow alleys were desolate and cool in the shadows. Walls crumbled where they faced the sea air. The more I walked, the more time I spent alone, the more the membrane between the inner and the outer world began to seem an illusion, the self just a collection of tricks, a series of black symbols on a page, a disembodied voice in my head.

Brando still called, and we still spoke. I had stopped telling him I loved him, but he seemed not to notice, barreling ahead with news from Baghdad. Amid the stories of car bombs and power outages, he remained optimistic. Maybe it was my state of mind, but I heard through all of it, understood beyond the hope in Wonderboy's staccato delivery, that everything was already lost.

One afternoon in late July, I set off on foot up the Bosporus road without a destination. It was a beautiful day and I thought the walk would do me good, release me from the paralysis I'd fallen into. I alternated between certainties, sure one moment that I had to leave the city and equally sure the next that I should be no place but here. Certain I should tell Brando everything and certain that it would be a mistake. Sure I should return to the States and convinced that the best thing I could do was to travel to Baghdad, risk everything, to see Brando again. I must see him again. I had to see his eyes when I asked him. But not before I packed. Maybe, if I really thought about it, I didn't have to leave.

I walked on like this, past the Dolmabaçe Palace, past the Çirağan, where Wonderboy and I had stayed on that first trip when we had been in love and happy, past Ortaköy. I walked all afternoon, in a half-dream, expecting to stop at the next village, but not having the strength to make the decision. It was very late in the afternoon when I found myself in Bebek, too far from home now and exhausted from the walk.

The Bebek hotel opened right onto the street. I had intended to walk past it, but the doorman held the door open for me and nodded with such assurance that I nodded back and went in. I walked through the darkened lobby and out to the deck, where I took a seat by the water and ordered a glass of *kırmızı şarap*.

Every table in the sun was occupied. The day was warm, but everyone seemed determined to avoid the shadows all the same. The Bebek had always had a problem with seagulls, and I sat for a while watching the waiters as they tried to force the birds off the railings. It was a frustrating and futile exercise for everyone, and after a while I stopped watching. I turned my seat to face the lobby. It was empty except for a woman in a black abaya who stood just inside the shadows, looking out.

At the next table, two American women were talking about the mad sultan Ibrahim, who in a fit of jealousy had ordered his entire harem drowned in the Bosporus.

"Only one girl survived," said the older woman. "The knot on her bag came loose, and she swam to shore."

"Lucky girl," said her companion.

The younger woman wore a white cloth hat that flapped in the breeze, and her voice was light.

Sailboats bobbed on the water, placid. Traffic backed up on the bridge, but on the other shore, in Asia, it was wooded and green. I was very far from home, though the word had come to mean less and less. The years I had lived in India had stripped me of the notion that one should belong anywhere. My mother tells of how, as a baby, I would begin to cry the moment the car turned onto our street for home. I read somewhere that "to learn to move freely about the world without longings or inventions takes years of patient learning." But I wonder if it's not the other way around. Maybe it's in our nature to fear return, to loathe the familiar, and it is only later that we learn that one is supposed to pine for the known. Civilization could hardly have survived without this idea of belonging, without an understanding of what is mine, what is yours, and what is theirs. Perhaps this is why travelers, unmoored and drifting like clouds, are so feared. The word in Turkish, *yabanci*, comes from the word for "strange," as it does in English and French. We imagine we can come to understand even the unknowable. But what we call reality begins and ends with language. Our little understanding, I know now, cannot reach beyond the limits of our two eyes and ears; our one mouth.

So I was strange and a stranger, as were Wonderboy and Mira, whoever she was. As were the two American women at the next table, describing Sultan Ibrahim and thrilling beneath their outrage at his penchant for furs and new sexual positions; marveling, without wanting to seem it, at the sultan's mad infatuation with his favorite harem girl, whose sex was said to resemble that of a young wild cow. It was she who had put the notion into his head that one of his concubines had been compromised by a stranger.

"Doesn't even matter if it was true," the older woman said.

She had a nervous laugh, and her hair was cut short. The other woman suddenly became serious and sad. She was thinking about something that she would never tell the other. I watched her for a long while until she shifted her gaze and met mine. After the two Americans left, I ordered another glass of wine. The sun had begun to set, and the wind changed. When it became too cool to sit out any longer, I paid the bill. I thought of calling Erkan, but ended up taking a cab back to the apartment. Night had come very quickly, and the road was dark and crowded. The driver had dense eyebrows, and his eyes kept darting beneath them, from the road, to the rearview mirror, to me. The trees by the Çirağan Palace had lost their color, and the streetlamps cast their gnarled shadows on the sidewalk; it hardly seemed the same road I'd taken earlier. How much could I be sure of?

I directed the cab to my house. *Sola dönün. Burada.* When finally we were in front of the Cili building, the driver turned around in his seat. He spoke to me intently. I understood nothing. He waited for me to respond and then repeated himself, patiently, forcefully. His words sounded like a warning. Or was it my nerves? "Is something wrong, sir?" I said. The man flicked his hand in the air. He tried one more time. I shook my head and checked the meter. I paid, intending to leave a generous tip. When I got to the front gate, I turned. The driver was inches from my face. I screamed and jumped back. He held out a few coins.

I took another step back, slowly this time.

The man spoke to me softly now, holding out the coins. He took a step closer. I pushed him, and he stumbled.

"Go away!"

The man watched me for a few more seconds. He took a half step toward me, and my heart raced. But then he stopped. He wrapped his fist around the coins and got back into his car. I waited until he'd pulled away, and then I reached around and opened the front gate. My hands trembled. The vestibule was dark and damp. I turned on the light quickly and raced up the stairs, not bothering with the cramped elevator. I reached the apartment with my heart pounding. I'd left the blinds open, and moonlight was coming in through the wide windows. I poured myself another glass—some of the unacceptable Turkish Gamay that I was beginning, out of necessity, to tolerate—and sat for a while looking out over the water. The moon was not quite full; the gulls circled the dome of the mosque. The teak table sat out on the terrace, the chairs in disarray. Had someone been in here? And who was the driver? Those moist eyes. I put down my wine and ran back downstairs. I reached the ground floor, panting. The doorman's door opened and then shut. The car was gone. Nothing but the old dog on the street corner.

I climbed back up to the apartment and locked the door. I took another sip of wine. I had to calm myself. I must not go down this way. How close madness was! I tried to think only of the moon, the silvered water, the mosque. But the letter. Who had written the letter? I went to the book where I kept it and opened it again. I read it quickly once and then again, more slowly, lingering over each word as if it were written for someone else. Mira. Who was Look?

My memory had never been good. Even as a child, I struggled to master the memorization that is so much a part of early education. To this day, I don't remember all my multiplication tables. Seven times eight? Nine times four? All that returns is a picture of my third-grade classroom. The teacher had bobbed hair, like Dorothy Hamill.

I blamed too much reading for my memory problems. If you could write anything down, what was the use of memory?

Once, we had memorized entire epics: *Rage—Goddess, sing the rage of Peleus' son Achilles, murderous, doomed, that cost the Achaeans countless losses, hurling down to the House of Death so many sturdy souls . . .* Our minds had been storehouses of great oratory, of secret knowledge. We committed entire histories to memory, contained whole worlds in one recollection. Now what? My mind, such as it was, was a collection of PINs and passwords with some advertising jingles thrown in, a few slights, some vague recollections of joy. Everything was fuzzy around the edges, not to be trusted. Had my marriage been happy?

I fell asleep on the couch, still in my clothes. Before dawn, I dreamed that my cell phone was ringing, and I woke, trembling, the phone silent. I went back to sleep, but fitfully, waking now and then. I dreamed of seagulls, their long dark shadows. Or did I imagine them, still awake? I was too tired to have slept. Reality frayed. My cell phone rang, but there was no one at the other end. I dreamed. I slept. I woke and knew I had not dreamed, the night just a dark well like any other. Over breakfast, I finally worried the source of my unease. Not the driver and his moist eyes. Before all that. At the Bebek, I had seen her again: the woman in the black abaya.

She had stood staring out over the deck—staring at me!—and then she had turned. I saw her face only briefly as she walked across the empty lobby and out the front door, bathed in the evening's blue light. I would not have dwelled on her under normal circumstances. It was unusual to see women in abayas on the European side of the city, but not without precedent. After September 11, more Arab families were vacationing closer to home—even at the home of the hated Turk—and once, in the Istanbul airport, I had seen a woman in the full blue burka of Afghanistan. So I didn't think much of the woman in the abaya right at that moment. It was only after she had passed through the lobby and out the door that something in her walk caught my attention. It was not an Arab woman's walk; she moved with the long ungainly strides of a Western woman who'd grown up wearing shorts and pants. It was her walk that I remembered. And I realized that I had seen the walk before, when I was leaving the tombs. I had waved to Erkan, who sat behind the wheel of the Mercedes. He flashed the lights and I crossed the street, narrowly missing a speeding cab. She had already crossed in the other direction. I had glimpsed her for just one moment before my thoughts were lost to Nadia's letters.

I finished breakfast and went into my office. I opened the window all the way and looked out into the street. I half expected to see her waiting there. But the street was empty except for an old man at his stoop and the big dog that always lay sleeping in the sheltered bend where the street turned up to the hill. I pulled the curtains closed. I must put the whole thing out of my mind, get back to work, decide what to do about the apartment.

I was not a hysteric, and I refused to act like one. But for the next few days, I wandered about the city in a heightened state. I was struck with a new sense of awareness, the certainty that there was more beyond the perceived. I felt myself sinking into that disorganized state when dreams cross into daylight. I became convinced that I had forgotten something important. I had so much to attend to, and the more I thought of it, the more disorganized my thoughts became. A magazine in Holland wanted to publish some of my photos from Afghanistan. But I'd shot that trip on film, and now I needed to track down the negatives, in storage somewhere, but where? I needed to make new prints, and for that I'd need to borrow a real darkroom. The thought exhausted me. I would talk to Wonderboy; he would know what to do.

So much time wasted! All those years of waiting for Brando to come home, to notice me, and nothing to show for it. Some crates of photographs, scattered notes. Why hadn't I organized myself, come up with a real plan? Did I think I could shoot assignments here and there forever? "What's your theme?" another photographer had asked me years ago. I had not the slightest idea what he meant. Your theme, he had insisted, the constant running through your work. Theme? I had no theme. My life was without theme, just waiting and wine. Working only so much as it suited me. Only war—only the clamor and noise of war made me feel alive. The drift, the constant yearning for the new and unexplored. Could that constitute a theme?

I would find a theme. Now was the time to find a theme. The years were passing. I pulled a chair to the hall closet and took down two boxes of old photographs. Surely there was a theme in there somewhere. Isn't that how it happened? You embarked on a life without plans, and then at the moment of your death, its theme flashed before you, the one idea organizing your fugitive life. I would find the theme. And if I couldn't do that, at least I would finally organize the photos. For years I'd been taking them and dumping negatives, loose prints, and then disks into boxes, always promising to get to them, establish order.

By nightfall, I had managed to sort just fifteen photographs— the only ones that I could be sure were from my first trip to Jaffna because of my overuse of the telephoto lens. Most were long shots of men on patrol, soldiers at roadblocks.

Near the end of the pile of photographs I came across a series that at first I thought belonged to another country— Pakistan perhaps, or northern India. Unlike the other photographs, these were of ordinary people, but I could remember nothing about them. I'd shot most of the photos with the wide-angle, the edges slightly distorted. Several photographs were of the same old man. In every shot, he stared into the camera, his eyes so clouded with cataracts that it was impossible to guess at whatever emotion lay beneath. His face was thin and dark. In some shots he sat very straight on a folding lawn chair. He wore a plain white T-shirt, and one long shot showed him wearing the traditional sarong of the countryside. When I saw that, I remembered where I'd shot the film.

In 1998, a mass grave was discovered in northern Sri

Lanka, and the country began to debate the terms under which the remains would be exhumed. I flew to Colombo with Wonderboy, where we booked at the old, rambling Galle Face Hotel. While he met with ministers and other important people, I took a little *tuk-tuk* through the streets—streets that always reminded me of home, with their overpowering green, their humid decay—to the small house that served as the headquarters of the Sri Lankan Association of the Missing and Murdered. The director was waiting for me at the door. She was plump and beautiful in a flowing sari, and only when she pressed my hand did I see that her eyes were sad. She had lost a husband to the government forces. He was either imprisoned or killed—she didn't know which—and she hadn't seen him in more than five years. She dealt with her sorrow by trying to salve that of others. That morning, she had gathered the parents of young men who had gone missing in the north for me to meet. I passed them waiting in a small room as she led me to a larger office where the old man was waiting. He was the first one I photographed. He spoke very softly of his son, beginning by telling me that he had always taken after the mother, with his narrow face and long arms. He and his wife had given up hope of having children until he came along, a gift. He told me this was his only son in all the world, and did I know what that meant? The man re-cited his story through a translator, his halting words turn-ing smooth and flat in the translator's voice. One morning, the son, not yet seventeen, had left to buy bread and never returned. The man spoke a long time about this, explaining that it had been a very hot day and the son had woken early. He told me about the little house. The store by the side of the road. If he had slept a little while longer? The son was lean and sad, the father protested; all he had ever known was war. Then the old man began to sob, long and deep, like nothing I had ever heard before, totally open in his despair. No, no, his son could not be in that grave; he was certain he was in a prison somewhere, locked up, wondering why his father had not come looking for him . . . He wiped his face and began to speak urgently. America is so powerful, everyone listens to America, if America wanted to it could fix this war, it could end all this suffering. Write it down, write it down, he commanded. And then he was quiet, exhausted from the effort. He is not dead, the man said after a while. I am sure of it. He leaned forward, his cloudy eyes fixed on me. You see, he said, the night before yesterday I dreamed that I held my son, his head in my lap, and I stroked his hair like I used to when he was a boy. The man closed his eyes and made the motions over his empty lap. Like this, I stroked his hair, he said. And it was so real, it was the most real dream I had ever had. And I woke so happy, you cannot imagine.

I shot the man's photograph as he spoke, three rolls of his grief.

I returned to the hotel late that afternoon and went to bed. We had a sea-facing room, and from the spot where I lay, I could see the sand and the palm trees and the blue sky and it was all so gorgeous. I closed my eyes and lay the rest of the afternoon, listening to the roar of the ocean.

I sat now for a while with the man's photograph in my hand. I remembered that the next day, Brando and I had traveled to Jaffna to look for the graves. Checkpoint after checkpoint was deserted. Finally, we came on a lonely outpost, and when no one came to open the wooden gate, we got off to look for the officers. We found them in a back room, gathered around a small television that had been hooked up to a generator. It was the World Cup finals, and the men would not be budged. We returned to the car and opened the gate ourselves. When we were a mile away, a tremendous explosion shook the ground. Years later, Brando retold the story to some friends. He'd forgotten all about the soccer match. All he could talk about was the sound. "You can't imagine it," he said over and over. "It was louder than anything you can conceive. Not like the movies—more like the end of the world."

I've heard soldiers say the same thing since. The young ones, especially, marvel at the force of the concussion, the report that obliterates even the heartbeat in your ears. I used to be impressed by this kind of talk. Like it was some kind of secret knowledge between men. Now it just seems sad and ordinary. Men at war always talk about the noise, as if by reaffirming the bang and flare of it, they might skirt the hole of lasting silence.

It was dark when I finished, and I was hungry. I couldn't decide what to do—I was too tired to cook and too tired to go out. I went into the kitchen and poured myself a glass of wine as I thought about it. I took out a block of cheese, but before I got to the table, I returned to the kitchen and put it away. The eyes in the photograph followed me past the door to the sink. Never blinking, watching. I drank my wine down and grabbed my keys and my purse.

At Rafik's there was a large crowd, unusual for a weekday, and I had to wait a long time for a table. When they finally sat me, it was upstairs in a corner by the kitchen. The waiter handed me the menu without looking at me and wheeled away. The dining room was crowded and warm. At the next table, a young man and woman argued loudly over something. I could understand only "You, you, you—*sen, sen, sen,*" repeated again and again. The evening was spoiled before I ever got my meze, and when it arrived, I picked at the grilled eggplant and cubes of white cheese. By the time the grilled fish came, I was no longer hungry. The fish was overcooked, as usual, and I left most of it on the plate. I set a couple million lira on the table and walked out. The cool night air was refreshing after the claustrophobic dining room, and I stood outside the door for a few minutes, gathering myself. The crowd had unbalanced me, and I fought the old feeling that I'd forgotten something important, again the sense of things left unfinished. I felt responsible, and I cursed myself for feeling it. I was the victim in all of this, no? I was the aggrieved party. I had nothing to be sorry for, after all.

I set off back home, up the hill following the trolley tracks. The stores had closed for the night, and only a few people were still out. I walked quickly, crossing side streets, barely watching for traffic. When I reached Taksim Square, I stopped. That last side street behind the mosque, the figure crouching. It was her, the woman in the black abaya. I ran back down along the tracks and turned onto the side street. The little road was narrow and dark, and it took some moments for my eyes to adjust. "You! Hey, you!" I called. It was definitely her, the same walk, now moving faster. She disappeared down another street. "Come back here! What do you want?" A woman opened a window above the alley and yelled something down at me, angry sentences that I didn't need to understand. I turned left at the next street and ran down the hill. Nothing. Two cats, darting ahead of the sound of my footfalls. Nothing more. In the distance, the report of a motorcycle racing up the hill.

I ran the rest of the way in my sandals and was sweating by the time I reached the apartment. I took the stairs two at a time. I opened the door slowly and waited a few minutes in the dark, listening to my breath. Then I stood and went into the kitchen and poured myself a glass of wine.

I needed to get home; it was crucial that I go home. I should be with my own people. Who had said that to me? Many years ago: *You should be with your own people.* I had found it terribly condescending. My own people. Who were my people? Why was someone always trying to shove you into last year's trendy bullshit about identity and belonging?

And yet . . . home. The familiar, a place beyond thought. I should get home. Wherever that might mean. I wanted something I could understand, a place where I might be accepted. The Istanbul apartment was cool, even in summer. The multitude of ordered, empty rooms did not have the give and play of life, the shared meals, the daily arguments, the awkward gropings toward love that reset time and let you wake with a sense that, if nothing else, at least there was meaning in the physical.

I would go home again. It could be done. I poured myself another glass of wine. It was not good for me, this isolation, the way I had gone on about the woman in the black abaya. It concerned me, this fixation. Was it a way not to think about the letter?

I should have worked harder. I should have had the forbearance that the nineteenth century gave to women. Instead I was a transitional model, the wife between social movements, unsure of herself at a time when certainty guaranteed power. A hundred years ago a woman of my age and class would be raising her children. What did it mean to question her happiness? Would she? All I would ever nurse was my own idleness, spinning out the years into a pattern that, unlike Penelope's, could never be undone or restarted.

I lay on the couch in the big room again, not able to face the ritual of bed, the fine sheets, the soft pillows that pointed not to comfort or ease but to the hollow, the place of the absent husband. I finally fell asleep toward dawn, but I had not found a comfortable position and dreamed shallowly of confinement and tangles; on the other side, a city burned, red sky flickering beyond the hills and the fire engines coming closer and closer, bells ringing. Bells ringing on the other side. I woke with my breath catching. I'd been asleep for less than two hours, but now I was fully alert above my exhaustion. I ran to the intercom and pressed listen. Nothing. "Who's there?" I flung open my office window. Warm, damp air. The early morning light was gray and thin. There was no one on the street.

I picked up the cell phone on the fifth ring.

"Tunes. It's me."

"Are you all right? Where are you?"

"I'm fine," Brando said. "Sorry to call so late. I wasn't able to get a line for the longest time. I don't know what's happened."

"It's like five in the morning."

"Oh, my God, I didn't realize it was that late. Can you believe I just filed?" he said. "Anyway, I'll be quick."

"What's the matter? Where are you?"

"I'm fine, I'm fine, don't be hysterical," he said. "I was just getting back to you on the AC."

"On what?"

"The AC."

"The what? The connection isn't very good. Where are you calling from?"

"Tunes," he said, louder now, "the AC, the fucking air conditioner."

Had I called Wonderboy to complain about the air conditioner? I had a vague recollection now, the AC in the bedroom. Was that why I had been sleeping out on the couch?

"It's not important," I said. My voice was unsteady. "I think it's working now."

"Look, I talked to Erkan yesterday," he said, ignoring me. "Why aren't you using him anymore?"

"What, did he complain?"

"He thinks he insulted you. At least, I think that's what he said."

"Oh, God. That's crazy. I just don't need him. I'm getting along fine without him."

"We're paying him, he's yours to use as you need," Brando said. "I made sure of that. I want you to be comfortable there."

"Thanks, that's kind of you."

"That's a nasty tone."

"I'm very grateful to you and the paper," I said, my voice flat, without emotion.

There was a long pause. Some static.

"Look," he said after a moment. "I can't talk long. Are you going to be home next week? Erkan's sending over some repairmen."

"My God, for what?"

"The air conditioner, Tunes."

"Oh."

"Oh?"

"I'll be here."

"Look, it was a pain in the ass to get him to understand what we needed. For what it's worth, the Turkish word is *klima*."

"Klima?"

"Word for air conditioner."

"Thanks. *Klima*—I'll remember."

"You OK?"

"Yes."

It was the first I'd heard from Wonderboy in several days. Now, with one call, he had pulled me in again. I knew it was the satellite phone, but he sounded really sick this time, like someone battling a chest cold. But there was something else besides. Not sadness, nothing so easy.

He'd warned me at the beginning. *Ah love, let us be true to one another.* He wanted to be a soldier, a man of daring. He could not escape the great-great-someone who had been a Civil War hero, the uncle wounded at the Battle of the Bulge. The parents who had met in Italy after D-day. In a glass box, he kept a bullet casing from the Romanian Revolution. War held him. I didn't know then that it also held me, the eldest daughter of immigrants who had conceived me in the dark, too far from home, memories of loss still more vivid than love's transport. Why had I imagined that it could be different the second time, that peace could have a place for us? Brando and I had been traveling for ten years, each new war spinning us farther out of reach. The edge was all we could maneuver now, the center had long since fallen away.

I should have left the apartment. I knew enough to know I was going mad by myself. But what if she was there, waiting? I knew the woman in the black abaya was looking for me.

There wasn't any doubt now. I knew the hour was coming when I would have to confront her. But not today, I couldn't today, please just a little more time.

Across the street in the next building, someone's maid was hanging out of a window, cleaning every inch of glass. I stood to lower the curtain and then stopped. Someone was walking slowly up the hill. The street was deserted except for this solitary figure. I leaned back a little in case she looked up, but my hand was still on the curtain. It was a steep hill, and she moved slowly. The effect was disconcerting, like an unburying. The woman came into view gradually, first the top of her veiled head, then the face, indistinct in the distance, and as the whole person finally emerged I saw that it was not a woman, but a young man with a scarf pulled high up his collar. He passed under the window, looking ahead the whole way, and then turned and continued up the other hill.

I went to bed early that night, but slept badly. Just after midnight, the sound of knocking woke me. I had not closed the curtains all the way, and when I opened my eyes, the streetlight was streaming in through the gap. It took me a few moments to remember where I was. And then another moment to understand what had woken me. I knew I should get up to look out the window, but I couldn't move. I lay very still, my ears tuned to every sound in that cavernous apartment. My mind, moving too quickly, rehearsed strange things: olives, *Why do you worry the infinite question?*, an e-mail I had never responded to, cashmere blankets, tarantulas . . .

The people upstairs were arguing again. The voices were muffled, but anger carries. Maybe they loved one another most of the time. But all I ever heard was the loathing. Their love was something conducted in secret whispers. Their hate demanded to be heard. Someone shoved a table, and a chair tumbled and scraped the floor. From one end of my ceiling to the other, the sound echoed. That must have been the knocking. I closed my eyes and breathed, letting my stomach fill and then letting all the air out. The last thing I heard before I fell asleep again was the sound of a woman sobbing.

I woke again to the first call to prayer. When the call stopped, a spot of light moved across my vision. I recognized it as the first visual disturbance of a migraine and sank back into my pillow. It had been five years since my last, and I knew I had brought it on myself, a guilt migraine for lying to Madam Rose.

The first minutes of a migraine are not bad, at least not compared to what comes after. In the first few minutes, it's still possible to retain a sense of control, or, more accurately, to imagine that such a thing is possible. You still hold the illusion of mastery over the pain, believing you may yet conquer it. That night, as the pain advanced, I made the handful of bizarre promises that make sense only under that peculiar state, willing the pain into retreat. The bedsheets were rough and the sliver of streetlight coming in through the curtains was now unbearable. I arranged my hair over my eyes and tried to sleep, or rather to lie still as if in sleep. When I woke for the third time that night, it was to stumble to the bathroom and throw up.

❊   ❊   ❊

In the morning, when I finally felt well enough to stand, I passed my reflection in the hall mirror and doubled back. I'd lost a lot of weight in the last weeks, and my cheeks were hollow and dark. The apartment, too, was bare. I had spent weeks hanging the paintings, setting out the rugs. But it was still a skeleton apartment, a stopping-place. It was as if the walls, the Bosporus, and the entire city beyond knew we were short-timers here, not worth wasting affection on.

The medicine cabinet held only a few pills, and most of those were expired. I found a bottle of chewable vitamin C with two tablets left. I took them both and put the empty bottle back on the shelf. The pills had softened and darkened in the humidity, but they were still tart.

I thought about it a long time, but eventually decided to go down to Istiklal in search of some Excedrin. It took me forever to dress, afraid as I was of upsetting the migraine with sudden movement.

Down on the street, the wind scarcely stirred. My senses sharpened by the migraine, I was able to detect, above the smell of diesel fuel, something burning in the distance.

I walked up the hill. It had rained during the night, and the street shone with oily puddles. I was out of breath as I approached Taksim Square, and it took me a few moments to realize that the roar I'd heard without hearing when I first stepped out of the apartment was getting closer and louder.

Or rather, I was getting closer to it. When I'd made it to the top of the hill, I saw the crowd that had gathered by the trolley tracks.

I stood in front of the Marmara Hotel to watch. There was no way I would wade into it, not with my head pounding. But as I stood debating whether to walk all the way to Maçka or take a cab home, a bigger crowd came up behind me from the stadium. They were war protestors, and most carried placards that read "Savaşa Hayır." Before I could act, I was carried along by the momentum, up toward the square. It was a jovial, fast-moving group, and I knew, without understanding, what they shouted. At the square, police wagons sat idling by the flower stalls. I lingered for a while, against my will, until I could free myself of the crowd and continue up Istiklal, chants of "Savaşa hayır, savaşa hayır" echoing behind me. The pharmacies by the square were all closed, and I had to walk far down near the fish market before I found a place that was open. I explained as well as I could what I needed, and after several minutes of confusion, the man disappeared behind the counter. He returned with a large dusty bottle of Excedrin. I checked it for the expiration date before handing him $25. "Su, su?" the man asked.

"Sue, what?" I said.

"Su," the man repeated, making a drinking motion. He disappeared into a back room and returned with a glass of water. "Ah, çok teşekkürler," I said. "I'm trying to learn Turkish, but it's very hard. *Çok zor.*" I swallowed two tablets and returned the glass. Even half comatose with migraine, I marveled at a culture that could gouge you for a simple painkiller and then demonstrate the delicacy of bringing you water to help you swallow.

I took the long way back, hoping to avoid the worst of the crowd, which I could still hear chanting in the distance. *Savaşa Hayır*. I had always read it as "No War," but now, in the postmigraine clarity, I realized I'd been leaving out the "to" implied in the final *a*. *No to War*. Turkish, Alif had tried to explain to me again and again, has no free-standing prepositions, instead deploying an army of infixes and suffixes that make for an ever-mutating dictionary. Nearly every word is transformed by its relationship to every other word. It's a hard lesson for an English speaker to grasp. The world formed by Turkish syntax is not the English one, where solitary objects move through the sentence with little cause or effect. Turkish exists in a webbed landscape where relationships carry meaning and every noun is malleable.

By the time I returned to the apartment, a light rain was falling. It wasn't enough to soak through my clothes, though, and the cool water felt good on my sore head. The medicine had started to work, and I was beginning to enjoy a little of the detached sense (almost elation) that, for me, always follows a bad migraine. I'd become quite taken by my new, fevered understanding of Turkish and was looking forward to putting my scattered insights down into some coherent form that might illuminate a bigger idea. I resolved again to sign up for some classes. The night seemed luminous: a half-stop beyond real. Under different circumstances, then, I probably would have noticed the figure in the courtyard much earlier. But it was already getting dark, and the thin rain and the pain had thrown a veil of light over everything. So it wasn't until after I had opened the garden gate and passed into the interior that I saw her. She was standing under the light, with her back to the door. She was still in the black abaya, though today she hadn't covered her mouth and the veil was pulled low over her head, exposing a section of dark, shiny hair. I felt complete calm. I remember that my only fear was that she would run away again. I closed the gate behind me and stood to block it, but the move was unnecessary. The woman had no intention of leaving this time. Before I could address her, she slipped off her veil and smiled broadly, throwing her hands in the air: "Flash, darling! It *is* you!"

Everything returned to me at once, and I knew that I had been here before, that I'd had a presentiment of this moment weeks ago. The images tumbling. All of it was suddenly familiar: the way I had opened the gate, the figure of the woman, the way her veil was pulled back, even the gesture she used when she spoke to me. Her hands were pale and small. She wore a ring with a blue turquoise, and I remembered that also. We didn't speak, and for what seemed a long while, neither of us moved. It had grown dark now, and a yellow streetlight cast its shadows. The woman's eyes were rimmed in kohl, but otherwise her pale face was free of makeup. Her lips were chapped. And then she smiled again, as if she had caught some recognition on my face.

"It is so good to see you, truly it is," she said.

I could not help a smile and then a laugh. "Alexandra Truso in Istanbul, I'll be damned."

She moved toward me and held both my hands, then gave me a hug. "I came by the other night," she said when she pulled away. "But you weren't in, and I didn't want to miss you this time. It is really marvelous, marvelous to see you."

"I'm sorry if I seemed rude," I said after a moment. "You startled me."

"I didn't mean to, truly," she said. "I can come back some other time."

I unlocked the front door and held it open behind me. "Not at all, come, get out of the rain."

I stepped inside, and she followed. We rode up to the third floor, rehearsing the usual lines: "It's been so long." "So good to see you." "You look well." The cramped elevator car smelled of rain and sweat. There was scarcely room for the two of us, and she had turned so that her profile was to me as she spoke. She took small, hesitant breaths, but her words were smooth and quiet. Inside the apartment, I quickly turned on the lights.

"It's a little ridiculous," I said, feeling suddenly that the huge space was an embarrassing indulgence. "All this for one person, but the view is great."

I opened the curtains so that the apartment was half reflected in the windows. It seemed at that moment to be floating over the Bosporus. The effect deepened the sense of superreality that had gripped me since I'd opened the gate and found Alexandra waiting there for me.

She walked to the window and stood staring out for a

moment. I watched her back rise and fall with the deep breaths. She turned to me. "It is a fabulous view," she said, and then added: "Just one person? So Brando is still in Iraq."

"He is," I said. "I'm waiting for my papers to come through so I can join him."

Alexandra nodded. "I'm waiting for mine also," she said. "So are a lot of other people. Istanbul has become hell's waiting room."

I smiled. "Let me get you some wine."

"Thanks," she said.

She slid off her veil and folded it into a neat square, then reached back and undid her hair, which fell now in dark waves around her shoulders. She didn't remove the black abaya, but I noticed for the first time that underneath it she was wearing jeans and sneakers.

"I see you haven't dropped the habit of going about in native dress," I said. "Though I should warn you that here in Istanbul there's no better way to mark yourself as a foreigner."

"Well, you know," she said. "More than anything, it's a way to be invisible."

"Isn't being a woman invisibility enough?" I caught the bitterness in my voice and immediately regretted it.

Alexandra looked at me, but didn't say anything. I went to the kitchen and opened a new bottle of wine, a Bordeaux I'd bought in duty-free and had been saving for Brando's return.

When I came back to the big room, I found Alexandra sitting on the couch, going through the photography book where I'd hidden the letter. I hurried over with her wine and took the book.

"So how long have you been following me around Istanbul?" I said, smiling to soften the edge of my unease.

Alexandra looked startled but then composed herself and took a sip of wine. She lifted her eyebrows and held up the glass.

"This is not Turkish," she said.

"French."

"Thank God," she said and took a long sip. After a moment she spoke. "In answer to your question, no, I haven't been following you around Istanbul," she said.

When I didn't respond, she continued. "I do think we've crossed paths a few times, but it wasn't until Istiklal the other night that I thought it might be you."

"Why'd you run away, then?"

"Did I?" she said. "I didn't think I had. . . . Well, I wasn't sure it was you. It was dark. And from a distance, you look like a regular Turk, you know."

"Come off it."

"Well, truth is, I was also worried about intruding," she said.

"What are you talking about, intruding?"

"I think the first time I saw you was at the tombs." She watched for my reaction. "Ah, I was right. It was you. You looked so sad that I didn't want to disturb you. I'd seen Isaac before he shipped out, and he told me Brando was already in Iraq, and I thought, well—"

"The tombs?"

"By the Blue Mosque," she said. "That was you, wasn't it?"

I took a sip of wine and looked at her.

"I was doing a project, nothing sad about that," I said. "You should have introduced yourself, though. I can hardly be expected to recognize you when you're wearing that get-up."

"Well, maybe," she said. "But I wasn't sure it was you. And anyway, those death places depress me."

"Depressing?" I said. "I just thought it was ugly."

"Well, that's a photographer for you," Alexandra said. "The only morality is the aesthetic. But it's different for the rest of us."

I was annoyed, but tried not to show it. "Oh," I said, "is it different?" I was watching Alexandra. A suspicion had slowly come over me.

"Yes," she said. "You know, for years I used to close my eyes when I passed cemeteries. I couldn't bear them."

"Cemeteries?"

"The dead," she said. "It seemed to me then that for all our talk of a living planet, it is really a dead one. The single generation of the living is nothing next to the countless generations of the dead, all those extinguished days piled end to end beneath us."

I was quiet for a moment. I had always hated her fancy talk.

"Or maybe we human beings just like to exaggerate our importance," I said.

She laughed. "Some of us, anyway."

Her eyes went to the book again.

"Alexandra," I said as evenly as I could, "did you write the letter? Are you Mira?"

As soon as I said it and saw her reaction, I knew she had no idea what I was talking about. A cloud of confusion passed over her face, which she instantly tried to hide. She wasn't guilty, just curious.

"The letter about what?" she asked.

"Never mind," I said.

"Oh, come on now, Flash, you can't do that to me, that's not fair. What letter did you think I wrote? You must tell me."

"It's not important," I said. "Just a poison letter."

"Ah," she said and watched me. "A letter about Brando."

"A letter about Brando," I said, the bitterness again seeping into my voice. God, how I hated that a voice was also capable of betrayal. I tried again, brighter. "A letter about Brando." But now I sounded obsessed. I said nothing more. And when Alexandra insisted on silence (an old reporter's trick that I always fell for), I said simply, "Yes, a letter about Brando."

I pulled the book of photography to me and opened it to page 123. I closed the book and handed Alexandra the letter. When she was done reading, she folded it up in thirds again and handed it to me without comment. I appreciated that. Appreciated, also, that she didn't try to do some stupid new-age thing like hug me or say, "Oh, Flash, how terrible." She just sat watching me for a few moments. There was neither pity, nor scorn, nor condescension in those black eyes. If anything, all I could detect behind her languid blinking was anticipation. Alexandra was first of all a writer, and this was a fascinating story. She could not help but be hungry for the rest of it.

"It's a pretty ordinary tale," I said. "Nothing to it. Happens a thousand times a day."

"Don't say that, Flash. A thousand times a day—what does that mean when what you're angry about is that it happened to you?"

Her eyes were turned down, in sympathy. But they shone, curious.

"I want to know who wrote it," I said.

"Don't you want to know if it's true?"

"First I want to know who, then I'll know if it's true."

Alexandra frowned and looked out the window. "Likeliest suspect is Nadia herself."

I hadn't considered this.

"Maybe," I said after a moment. "But she's too much of a do-gooder to deliberately inflict pain."

Alexandra arched an eyebrow, but remained silent.

"Moralizers have no problem breaking the rules and sneaking around when they know they aren't going to be caught," I said. "They have all sorts of ways of justifying what they do to themselves—or forgetting it entirely. But most of them usually stop short of active malice."

"So you know her, then." Alexandra was grinning, but there was something old and hard behind her eyes. I shifted in my seat, unable to meet her eyes.

"Not really," I said. I was ashamed of my midnight googling.

"Oh," she said.

"I know of her."

"Who does she work for?"

I suddenly realized that there was a chance Nadia and Alexandra might have run into each other in Afghanistan.

"I have no idea," I said.

"I'm sorry," she said. Her face had assumed its old neutrality, and the hardness in those black pupils filmed over again with simple curiosity. "It's an awful letter. And racist on top of everything."

"Racist? Really, you think?"

" 'Artists of color'? Come on, no one talks like that anymore but freaks."

I laughed.

Alexandra raised her glass. "To us artists of color," she said and made a face.

I drank my glass down.

" 'Identity's just a role we play in public,' " Alexandra said. "I don't remember who said that."

"Some reactionary," I said.

"Nah. Chinese poet, if I recall."

"Yeah, well, what the hell does he know."

Alexandra smiled. "You seem in good spirits, in spite of things."

I shrugged. "Just making nice for company. Old habit."

"You still shooting?"

"Yes. And I know you're still with VOA. I catch the broadcasts now and then."

"Yeah, and still hating it," Alexandra said. "But what's the alternative for people like us? Some boring marriage in some boring suburb?"

"Marriage isn't so bad," I said automatically.

"Flash, darling . . ." Alexandra trailed off. "What are you going to do to track down this anonymous crow?"

I shrugged again.

"Does Brando know?"

"About the letter? God, no. I thought of telling him, but it's easier for him to lie over the phone. I want to wait until he's back."

Alexandra stood and began to pace.

"I can call up some people in Amman and put them on the case," Alexandra began.

I held up my hand. "Please, Alexandra. Not a word of this to anyone," I said. "I don't want this getting out. At least not before I have a chance to ask Brando about it in person. OK?"

Alexandra nodded.

"Please, Alexandra, I'm serious," I said. "I'm a private person."

She looked at me steadily. Her eyes were dark and clear. "You're ashamed."

I stood. "Ashamed?"

"Ashamed," she said evenly.

"Ashamed?" My sudden anger surprised me. I stood and began to pace. "I have absolutely nothing to be ashamed of. Ashamed? As if I were the one who did something wrong.

You don't know what you're talking about. What do you know of my life? What do you know of what it's like to get something like this?"

Alexandra sat back and stared at me, calm, assured, the way I had always known her to be. I turned away.

"I didn't sleep all that night," I said. "Do you know what it's like to cry and cry and cry? I cried until I had no tears left. And for what? The worst thing is what a fool I felt. There's never just one time, there's just the one time you find out about. All those trips Brando was always taking, quick trips, no photos, in and out. Those odd connections through Dubai, where he would always, because of one airline screwup or another, be forced to spend the night. Don't talk to me about ashamed. Destroyed, bereft, that's what I am. All those plans we made. Goddamn it, Alexandra, he used to send me postcards of old couples and write: 'That's how we'll be, toothless, but in love.'"

I had started to cry.

Alexandra sat very still. There was nothing like sympathy in her eyes, only a cold hard judgment. After a moment, she stood. I thought she would touch me, but she walked slowly to the window and stood staring out for a while.

"Betrayal is the most painful blow," she said. "Maybe more painful than death. It takes so much to love, such a terrible leap. It's illogical and stupid, and only a fool would leave herself stranded in a strange country knowing all that she has to lose. That intensity of feeling—that ends up exposing you to the worst cruelty."

Now she turned and faced me.

"I don't have anything to tell you that you don't already know, Flash. I sometimes wonder if they don't go about it better in the East, what with the arranged marriages and the instant love affairs."

I sighed, still remembering. "They have their own sorrows, I suppose," I said, and wiped my face.

"Maybe." She stopped and looked at me. I poured her another glass.

"Yes," she said.

After a while, she cleared her throat. "A man I was once very close to told me a story."

She paused and searched my face. "He was about fourteen years old at the time, and he and his family were living in Peshawar, in exile."

"Please, Alexandra."

"Listen," she said.

I said nothing.

"One day, leaving the bazaar," she continued, "he passed a *haveli*, and something moved him to look up. There in the upper windows, her face partly obscured behind the glass, stood a beautiful girl. He could not move from his spot. He was in love. Just like that. Does it sound strange to you?"

"Why would it?"

"That kind of sudden attraction—it's not the way we do things in the West, where love is some kind of dreary, drawn-out job interview."

"It's not that, necessarily," I said.

"No," she said, her dark eyes on me in the old way. "I don't suppose so. Anyway, the girl, being no doubt a nice Pashtun girl, quickly moved away from the window. She probably wasn't supposed to be there anyway, you know. Idiotically bold, what she was doing. Maybe she was a free spirit herself. Decided, Who says I shouldn't stand by the window on this lovely day, and whoever sees me, sees me. But then this young man appears, and all her bravado must have slipped. Maybe she was horrified at what she'd done."

"Horrified?" I said.

"Also thrilled. Sometimes it's the same thing," Alexandra said. She looked at me before continuing, as if changing the subject. "The next day, this boy walked by, and there she was again. Just for a bare second. But he saw her. And then he knew that she had wanted to be seen."

"So he went back," I said.

"The next day and the next and the next," Alexandra said. "And each time she gave him the barest smile and moved back into the shadows."

"He should have dropped the whole thing," I said angrily.

"Maybe," Alexandra said, smiling. "But instead he sent a note through one of the servants—an unfathomable act. It was returned to him unopened. He sent another. And another. By this time he was completely obsessed. He didn't want anything else in the whole world but this girl he had never met, never really seen, didn't know, had never spoken to. It was a kind of religious ecstasy. That's how he described it. That's why it didn't seem odd to him. We would call him a stalker, unbalanced, repressed. But he was just a seeker after the one pure thing—the perfect love that a man has for his god."

"Give me a break," I said.

"Stay with me, Flash, because this story is really about the young girl. The truth is, she had contempt for her lover. The only thing that animated her life was appearance. Her mother had surely warned her against this sort of thing. But she had gone and done it anyway and hadn't thought about whether it was right or wrong until she faced the possibility of getting caught. You see, the guilt provided its own kind of emotional intensity. Its own pleasure."

I sighed. "So let me guess, the boy stopped eating."

"And studying or sleeping—all he could think about was this girl," Alexandra continued. "So one night, after lying awake for hours, he dressed and ran all the way to the *haveli*. He stood beneath the window shouting his secret name for the girl. The dogs started barking. A servant came out. But no light came on in the house, anywhere. The *haveli* was a dark blank mountain. He shouted and no one answered but the elderly servant, who pleaded with him to go home to his parents."

"He knew it was lost. But he couldn't live without this girl. So he took out the razor he brought and slashed his forearms, each slash, crying out the girl's name. Seven slashes on the left, three on the right."

"You counted," I said.

"I did."

I tried to act as if nothing, but sweat had begun to bead above my lip.

Before she left, Alexandra wrapped the veil tightly around her head. She kissed me on both cheeks.

It wasn't until she was gone that I wondered what—or whom—she was running from this time.

Chapter 10

The next morning I woke, for the first time in days, without pain. But something nagged at me, some reminder that I shouldn't be altogether free, and then I remembered Alexandra's visit. I thought it might have been a dream, one of those diaphanous migraine confabulations. I remembered the way the apartment had seemed to float on the Bosporus, the silent elevator ride down, the way the hem of her black abaya had flapped in the still night, without sound. Then I walked out into the big room and saw the second glass of wine on the floor where she'd left it, untouched.

It happens that certain people, like certain stories, linger deeper in the mind, sometimes lying still and hidden in a place inaccessible even to the warp of memory. When they resurface suddenly, in a gesture, a sound, we may recognize them not as a part of our own history, but almost as a shared memory that transcends even the boundaries of experience. I know now that Alexandra and Afghanistan will forever be one for me, not for reasons of place and time, but for their shaping of an entirely new self.

I had known Alexandra since the early 1990s. Brando and I had first met her in New Delhi, where she was living with her husband, a Brit who worked for the BBC. Alexandra and I became fast friends in the way that is possible only for expats, who, for all their worldly pretensions, can't help gravitating to their own in foreign places. She was the American-born daughter of a British father and a Spanish mother—steeped from birth in the fluid identity that creates travelers and writers. When Wonderboy and I first met her, she had just published a slim book of short stories that had won her some modest notice. Her husband, Derek I think his name was, was good-looking and thin, fey in that British way, a man who seemed to prefer work to almost anything else. He was rarely in Delhi, and if Alexandra resented it, she didn't show it. She held regular dinner parties, and Brando and I made it a point to stop there whenever we were in town.

Alexandra wore elaborate silk saris to these parties and sat regal and calm in a white leather chair. She was one of those women who seemed more beautiful the second time you met them, some combination of personality and bearing that I have always admired and tried, without success, to emulate. Her eyes were large and slightly slanted. Her hands were small, pale, and slender, and she used them to great effect. She seemed in perpetual good spirits, and I was drawn to her immediately. She was a few years older than me, and as I sat in those parties, tongue-tied and unsure of most of what was being said, I envied her that worldly looseness, her calm assurance. Her father had been in the foreign service, and Alexandra had grown up in half a dozen cities. Later, I would come to recognize others in her tribe, and eventually I would become a hesitant, somewhat incompetent member myself. But back then I was too young to see through the chameleon's act that all successful drifters have perfected, that ability to instantly absorb a culture's shorthand—be it a gesture, a phrase, a way of dress—so as to hide in it. It's a genteel sort of self-destruction, though by the time one realizes what's happening, it's usually too late.

She and Derek lived in a rambling house in one of Delhi's most fashionable neighborhoods. Brando and I had rented a flat in the flashier South Delhi expat ghetto of Vasant Vihar, a short cab ride away. A photographer's work is finished much earlier than a reporter's, and late afternoons, when Brando was only beginning to write, I would sometimes leave him and have the driver take me to Alexandra's. She always greeted me as if we had been girlhood friends. "My dear," she said, in what I took to be a sly parody of her husband. "So lovely to see you." Derek was rarely about, and when he was, he stayed in the office or read, sprawled on an easy chair, as Alexandra and I chatted amiably away.

By the time we all met again in Afghanistan, no one was surprised to learn that Alexandra had left both Derek and book writing behind to embark on a new career in radio. By then she was traveling in the company of a young Afghan translator, a beautiful Pashtun boy whose attentions she delighted in flaunting. "My dear," she said to me during the long ride through the desert, "marriage was at its best when it was just a simple business contract. Ever since love got mixed up in it, the institution has been on a collision course with itself."

I didn't know what she meant then and put it down to good-humored disenchantment. Later, Alexandra would refer to Derek as "that charming thief," and I came to understand that she meant she had left him before he could finish stealing whatever was essential and wild in her.

Chapter 11

After a quick breakfast, I set about organizing the apartment. Books were scattered all over, and New York was sending magazines faster than I could read them. I gathered them all up in disgust and threw them in a bag. Next I went through my closet and filled another bag with clothes I didn't need. I made plans again to leave Istanbul. What was I sitting around waiting for?

I sat down to draw up an inventory of the things I would take with me. The list-making consumed a good part of the afternoon—rugs, china, paintings, and a detailed list of books and music. By two o'clock, I was starving and, deciding I'd had enough of the inside of the apartment, I set off for Istiklal. I had managed to put Alexandra out of my mind and was glad to be outdoors. The rain had passed, and now the sky was blue and deep, the day warm. Istiklal was crowded, as it usually was after a storm—all those people eager to get out finally and walk in the sunshine. I went to the café at the end of Tünel and ordered the same sesame chicken salad and sat and read and drank coffee until it was almost dusk.

I'd intended to walk straight home, but on the way back up Istiklal I passed a luggage store and went in.

Purses and bags hung from hooks along the walls from floor to ceiling, and the store smelled of soft leather. As soon as the door closed behind me, a man stepped out of the back room and stood behind the counter, watching me. I've probably disturbed his supper, I thought. I smiled and greeted him. It was the polite and proper way to enter stores in Turkey. He nodded and greeted me back. An entire life can be consumed in the detailing and retaining of such niceties. And what of it? What was the alternative? I browsed for a few minutes and then returned to the counter. "I'm looking for a big bag, not expensive," I said. The man nodded and led me to a corner piled with nylon bags. He stood over me as I crouched down to go through them. After a time he spoke in English. "Going home?" he asked.

I paused a moment before responding, "Yes, I am."

When I'd paid, he reached beneath the counter and drew out a little toiletry bag. Without making a fuss, he tucked it into the bigger bag. "A gift for you," he said gravely. "For the small things."

When I got back to the apartment, the people upstairs were at it again. Usually they screamed at one another in Turkish that I could not understand. Sometimes, as today, they shouted in French, which I could understand a little better. The man shouted over and over again, "Parce que tu, oui, tu." And she responded with something I couldn't hear well

enough to make out. Her crying, though, was clear and un-
mistakable. She began to sob and something hit the floor and
skidded across. There was some scrambling over the wooden
floor and then what sounded like a struggle. This went on for
several minutes. I stood motionless in the vestibule, holding
my bag. Then a glass broke and everything was still above.
I waited a few moments. Silence. I set my bag down finally
and went into the kitchen to pour myself a glass of wine,
which I drank quickly at the kitchen table.

In the master bedroom, I turned on the air conditioner.
The blast of hot air reminded me it was broken. But I left it
on. At least the fan worked. The bag was made of thin nylon
and shaped like a sausage—the kind of bag you use once
just to get out of town. I emptied my dresser drawers into it,
socks, T-shirts, underwear. When I was done, I moved on to
the top shelves of the closet, filling the bag with sweaters and
a collection of silk saris that I'd forgotten about.

I was glad I had made up my mind. I would go home
now. I had never been so sure of the rightness of anything.
I was letting my life run out here. I packed frantically until
nothing more fit into the suitcase. Then I zipped it up and
shoved it across the floor. I left it beneath the window, where
it would be out of my way. Yes, I'd move back to Miami. I
had family there, and some friends. It wouldn't be so bad.
And how would I support myself? What would I do for
money? This question made me sit down on the bed. The
sureness I had felt moments earlier was replaced by a vague
fatigue. Could I really move, leave everything? Leave what?
There was nothing for me here, not even a husband. I could

find work somewhere, even if it was photographing weddings or, as a very last resort, working for the paper. It wasn't such a big deal, lots of people did it. I remembered Alexandra's words.

Oh, God, but to live in one place until I died? A three-bedroom house in the suburbs with neighbors and a lawn to mow? At least there was honor in that. What honor was there in my life now? Living beyond my means in a place that would never be mine, cynically pampered by my husband's employer. How long would that last? And me in control of nothing. No, I would go home. Definitely I would go home.

I went on like this for a while until I grew too exhausted to continue the arguments. I lay staring at the ceiling, and after a while, without willing it, I fell asleep. I woke just before five to the call to prayer. I lay in the dark for a few minutes, disoriented. Upstairs, someone shoved a chair across the floor. I turned on my side and saw a dark bulk below the window. The room closed in on me. You stupid woman, you left the front door unlocked when you walked in, so concerned with your eavesdropping, and now something's come to crouch in the shadows. I forced myself to sit up in bed, my heart beating in my throat. I opened my eyes and closed them, but when I opened them again, the figure was still there, a dark mass below the still-darkened window. I had no one to call, I was alone. Then the call to prayer ended, and as if a spell had been lifted, I remembered the suitcase.

But now I was awake, and nothing would make me close my eyes again. I stood quickly, the movement making me momentarily dizzy, and ran to the front door. I had, in fact, left it unlocked, and the hidden memory of it must have been playing in my mind as I slept. I turned the lock now and jumped at the sound it made, like a gunshot that continued to echo down the steep empty stairwell beyond the door. I walked through the apartment turning on every light in the house. I opened closets and stood listening for stray sounds. Nothing. The couple upstairs must be sleeping off their argument. By the time I returned to the big room, the sun had already begun to rise over the hills. I made some coffee and took it out to the terrace.

The light that morning was weak and gray, and as it swept away the night, it replaced it with nothing better.

Chapter 12

It had been Brando's idea to travel to Afghanistan. For weeks, I told him I wouldn't be able to go, it was too dangerous, too hot, too-too. But at the last minute, I changed my mind and flew to meet him in Peshawar, where we were to meet up with another group of journalists and our Pashtun fixer. Wonderboy got me the way he always got me: This may be your only chance to see the country, you want to miss it?

We drove in two cars across the Khyber Pass—a romantic name made less majestic in its hot, dusty reality—and switched drivers at the border. The drive took sixteen hours. I was near delirious with hunger and fatigue by the time we pulled into the outskirts of Kabul near midnight. Perhaps this accounts for my vivid impressions of that night, of the silent blackness and the Big Dipper balanced just above the dark mountains, as if a great cataclysm had sent it hurtling down from heaven.

The next day was Friday, when the people traveled to the sports stadium after prayers to watch the executions. It had been a brilliant day, blue and warm. After, we drove back through the gutted streets to the hotel. I noticed for the first time that all the windows in our room had been shot out. That the thin brown blankets on the twin beds scratched the skin. Hours later, I lay alone in my narrow bed, still exhausted awake. The boy had walked out to the field under his own power. He'd left as a hooded body flung onto a flatbed truck. Brando snored softly in the next bed. I was filled then with a terrible fear and loneliness and a sudden deep, desperate desire. I wanted to cling to him, never leave his side. The line between fear and love had never seemed so thin.

A week later, we flew to Kandahar. There, in the ruined city, Alexandra appeared again. She was dressed in a blue burka when I first saw her, striding across the courtyard at the guesthouse like a burlesque ghost, her slim white wrists gesturing in the old way.

I was sitting on the grass with Wonderboy and Patrice, and both men looked up at the sound of a woman's voice. When she was a few steps from us, she flung the burka off dramatically and Patrice—rogue Frenchman that he was—couldn't suppress a small groan of approval at the jeans-and-T-shirt-clad woman before him. Alexandra was still beautiful, with an even more firmly entrenched confidence that deepened her charm. I noted that Wonderboy moved a little apart from me at her approach. Had it always been like that?

I jumped up to hug her, and I was followed by Brando. Patrice remained sitting on the grass, switched his cigarette to his left hand, and offered up his right hand, which Alexandra ignored. She was absolutely delighted, my dears, to see us.

I had not seen Alexandra in almost five years, but she was

the same woman she had always been. Everything that in me was ordinary, in Alexandra was magnified to rarity. The dark hair and eyes that rendered me anonymous in the countries we traveled, in Alexandra seemed exotic and captivating. Even when she was tightly wound in her native dresses, men could not help but look at her.

"They told me some other Americans were here, but never in a million years could I have guessed it was you two," she said, taking one of my hands and one of Wonderboy's.

"Oh, marvelous, my dears, just marvelous." She was careful to divide her gaze evenly between us.

After a while, we moved inside for tea. Alexandra told us she had moved to Kabul with the idea of freelancing radio. But she soon discovered it was far more lucrative to get herself hired out to visiting film crews as a fixer. She knew enough Pashto to make arrangements and she was in good with the leadership, a happy consequence of her affiliation with her young man. She was living in Kabul, and had arrived in Kandahar on Monday, ahead of a Japanese team that was making a documentary on the Taliban's rise to power.

We drank our tea and listened to Alexandra. Now and then Patrice asked her a question, which she answered with curt politeness until he finally stood and left. Brando said little, but I saw him watch her hands, the way she gestured.

Later, after dinner, Alexandra and I went back out to the courtyard to smoke. The pomegranates were in season, and they dotted the trees like ornaments. She turned to me and said, "Flash, my dear, so are you happy?"

❧   ❧   ❧

The next morning we were picking up yet another group of journalists and the television crew from Japan before caravanning it up to Herat. We woke before sunrise, with the stars still out. It was September, and the drive through the desert would be worse as the day wore on. I left the details to Wonderboy and went out to sit in the courtyard, where it was cooler. I watched the sunrise from there, pale through the dust and haze. The UN guesthouse was the only place for foreigners to stay, and for a while I had the courtyard to myself. It was still early. The little I had seen of Kandahar the day before was grimy and hot. But the guesthouse was surrounded on all sides by high walls that kept out the noise and menace of the street.

I sat on the grass, reading—I had carried Hopkirk's *The Great Game* with me from Peshawar. Those guys hadn't waited around for visas and fixers; they hadn't complained about the food or the lack of air conditioners. That was a time of real bravery, all really sustained by a pure and unselfconscious imperialist ambition. After about an hour I looked up to find two young boys heading toward me with a plate of flatbreads and a bottle of jam. They were giggling and jostling each other. The boys had led us to our room the previous night, and I had assumed they were sons of the man who ran the guesthouse. But it turned out they were war orphans. How they'd gotten themselves attached to the guesthouse, I didn't know. Afghanistan then was full of orphans from the many wars. The hungry boys roamed the streets, full of wile.

They could offer a shoeshine and beg for errands in several languages. These two must have been especially charming or sad cases to be taken in by the United Nations. The boys had stopped giggling by the time they reached me. The older one handed me the plate of breads very solemnly. "Happy breakfast, Mrs. Mister," he said. And then they both ran off, overcome with giggles again. "Thank you," I shouted after them. They crouched at the far end of the courtyard to watch me.

The bread was still warm—something I might not have noticed in any other setting. But here where so much was broken and impossible, the gesture seemed filled with grace, and I ate slowly and with gratitude. The boys had picked up a stick and were taking turns boring into the dirt with it. Now and then they gave out shrieks of delight. I smiled and waved when they looked up at me. The warm bread, the boys' laughter, the early morning coolness under the pomegranate trees—it all helped erase the memory of the execution. Not erase, perhaps, nothing is ever completely erased. But the sense of hopelessness—the feeling of sad loneliness that the execution had left me with—gave way a little to the order of a new day. That boys who had seen so much destruction could still giggle was proof that the world could repair itself. The older one had his arms around the little boy, and as he poked in the dirt the younger boy's face would fill with wonder and then delight all over again. After a while, the older boy handed the stick to the younger one and they continued their game. I finished the bread and set the plate on the grass, not wanting to interrupt the boys. It was almost eight in the morning by now, and the city had begun to wake beyond the walls. There was the sound of loud talking, and now and then a truck motored by. At one point I thought I heard a siren. I had decided to wrap myself up and go look for Brando when the boys' shouting caught my attention. The older one had the stick again and he was flinging it about with relish. The little boy was jumping up and down beside him. But for the first time I caught something else in their shouts, something abandoned and wild. The older boy had a peculiar concentration, and I stood suddenly. When they saw me, they stopped and then began shouting at once for me. I hurried to them and was immediately sick. They had not been playing innocently amid the pomegranate trees; they'd been torturing a baby leopard gecko that now lay half on its side, its severed tail in the dirt. I grabbed the stick from the older boy. I had meant only to scare him, but after the first whipping across the legs I couldn't stop. I hit his calves again and again, shouting at him, "Bad boy, bad, bad." The little one ran off, but the older boy just stood there, taking my beatings. He said nothing and didn't even flinch, only looked at me with big eyes. I don't know how long I went on beating him. Then there was shouting and I looked up to see the little one running toward me with the cook behind, screaming something. I stopped and flung the stick away from me. The cook was a thin man who came up to my chin, but he shouted at me now, clapping his hands in front of my face for emphasis. I shouted back in English about the gecko and all you sick bastards in this godforsaken shit country. The noise drew the others from their rooms, and soon we were surrounded by a small crowd arguing and shouting in several languages. I looked around. Wonderboy and Alexandra were nowhere. I left the courtyard and went to our room and threw myself on the bed. After a while I heard knocking, which I ignored. It went away, and then a few minutes later, the knocking returned, this time louder. I didn't move from the bed.

"Tunes, it's me."

"I'll be out in a second."

"Let me in," he said.

I did nothing.

"Tunes, man, what's the matter with you? What happened? Will you let me in?"

I stood and opened the door. A small crowd had gathered in the courtyard. Patrice and Miles stood talking to three of the Japanese journalists. Behind them stood an Afghan boy of about nineteen, looking straight into our room.

"What the hell were you thinking about?" Wonderboy said as soon as he came in the room. Patrice was walking toward us. I closed the door with a bang.

"I'm going home," I said. "I don't want to be here anymore. I don't feel well. I don't understand anything, everything is disorder. I'm going home. I'm not staying."

Wonderboy stood staring at me for a moment and then spoke very slowly. "You can't go home. There's no way to go back now," he said.

"Of course there is, don't be melodramatic," I said. "I'm getting out of here."

"You can't," he said.

"I can hire a car and drive to Quetta."

"Here, sit down," Wonderboy said. "Have a drink of water."

He waited. "Tunes, the next flight is in two days and it's too dangerous for you to go by yourself overland."

"I don't give a damn about the danger," I said. "I'm going home."

Brando sat next to me on the bed and took my hand. "It's going to be OK, Tunes, we're together. Nothing's going to happen to you as long as we're together. I love you, Tunes. You'll be OK. We'll spend a few days in Herat, and then we'll fly out of here. We can get on one of the UN flights to Peshawar."

"Those nasty boys were torturing a lizard," I said.

"Tunes, man, cut them a break," he said. "They're just boys."

I stood and grabbed my veil. I wrapped it around my head and put on my sunglasses. "I can't wait to get the fuck out of this fucking country."

It was noon by the time the convoy was ready, much too late. Miles was smirking when I walked out to join the others. "Hey, mate, you can't beat on the orphans," he drawled, exaggerating his Australian accent. "Only the Taliban gets to do that." Patrice, standing behind him, laughed.

"It's late," I said, setting my face hard. "We won't get to Herat until dark."

Patrice shrugged. He was smoking again. "So, that is nothing," he said. Patrice and Miles had driven out with us from Peshawar to Kabul. On the road through the gorge,

Patrice had smoked Camel after Camel, all the while saying it was nothing, Afghanistan was nothing. Fear was nothing. The Taliban, they were nothing. All the world was emptiness. He'd gone on and on in this way until Brando had turned around from the front seat and said, "Give it a rest, Sartre." Even Patrice had laughed.

We were to travel in five cars, and after another twenty minutes of shuffling, Miles and Patrice joined the Spanish in the big truck, and Alexandra and her translator ended up with us.

I was sitting in the front seat with Brando, but the driver complained, and I moved to the back with Alexandra and the boy.

They sat close together, whispering and smiling. When I bent forward to tell Wonderboy something, I noticed that beneath the folds of her scarf, Alexandra and the boy had joined hands. The car bucked and slid on the rutted road. The windows were opened, and the wind was very warm. We drove for miles, the car moving like a strange creature on the moon, the only sound Alexandra's whispering and the *slap slap slap* of the soporific wind.

Chapter 13

A red cargo ship moved down the Bosporus. I could just make out the Cyrillic writing on the hull. It was moving very slowly, but even so it disturbed the waters. A small white boat bobbed and fussed in its wake. And then the ship passed into the mouth of the Marmara, and everything was calm again. The small boat floated near the banks for a few minutes, and then it righted itself and continued its course, a prudent distance behind the ship. It was a windless morning, and the water, after the ship had passed, was utterly flat. Someone had told me that a reverse current ran deep beneath the surface of the Bosporus, and even on still days it was strong enough to catch fishing nets and carry a trawler back upstream to the Black Sea.

In the last year, I had slowly begun to sell off my old photography equipment and replace it with digital. In the newsrooms, photographers were still saying the technology would never be good enough. But in the field, we knew the business was only going to get easier and faster. Of course, digital is not the same as film: the layers are gone; flat pixels can't replace the richness of film. But digital has the advantage on the battlefield of being easy and fast. I updated my equipment slowly, cursing the technology but buying into it. I bought a new Canon, learned the software. Ditched the old IBM for an Apple. I worked almost exclusively in digital now, though I had never gotten used to it—there was something airy and unreal about it. If it weren't for the obsession, the need to press forward that I didn't understand but nevertheless succumbed to, I would have abandoned the whole enterprise, gone into flower arrangement or some other old thing. But I was still a photographer, not for any grand reason. It was just all I knew. Some days it seemed worthless. Who would ever really see these moments as I had? Who could know what I meant to say? And other days it seemed like the only thing that mattered. Like today, with that red ship sailing like a beacon in the weak blue light of morning.

I sat down with the magazines to wait for the repairmen. In the afternoon, when they still had not shown, I took the letter out again to reread it. All alone in Istanbul. Was that a threat? What did it mean? For all the supposed dangers of living abroad, I had rarely felt vulnerable. Suddenly, I was aware of how alone I really was. These repairmen. Who were they? How long should I wait? What was proper? And what was I still doing in this country?

I remembered a story a friend had told me. Her mother lay dying of throat cancer. She was out of breath for the last week of her life, every expression an agony. Her last words were labored and precise, as valuable as a beggar's last pennies. My friend pressed close to listen. "So this was life," her mother had whispered through the pain. "What a pointless exercise."

Chapter 14

Saturday morning. I woke to the recorded singsong of the gas truck, Asgaz! The dog on the street corner lifted his head to look and then let it drop again.

I walked uphill past the Japanese consulate. When had the barricades gone up? Across the street, the windows gleamed on the Beaux Arts buildings. They were gorgeous, but Brando and I had visited friends there, and the inside had been filthy. Past the Chinese restaurant with the garish pagoda. A woman selling plastic trinkets beneath the red arches. A few yards away, a policeman stood, rifle ready. By the Marmara Hotel, a thin and dirty man sat hunched behind a sign that read "Çok Açım." Inside, the fashionable sat down to pastries and tea.

At Taksim, a crowd waited for a trolley. Teenagers walked in groups. Day, at last. The sun warmer than it had ever been. And no one gave me a second glance. If I wasn't a foreigner, what was I?

❀ ❀ ❀

At Kahvehaus, the doors were open and there was an empty table by the window. The trolley stopped and rang its bell. I sat, ordered an espresso, turned, and there, in the doorway, stood Alexandra. She waved and, without waiting for me to say anything, took the chair opposite me. She was wearing the black abaya, and a few women in the café turned to give her a nasty look. Alexandra didn't seem to notice. She arranged her veil with one hand as she summoned the waiter with the other. "Bir büyük kahve." The waiter smiled at her, as all men did eventually, and responded in English, "One large coffee, madam, of course."

Alexandra turned to me and without preamble said, "I've been thinking about your situation, my dear Flash, and I've determined that what you need is a younger man."

I flinched, and Alexandra noticed.

"Did I say something bad?" she said.

I stared at her. "I'd rather be alone," I said.

"Of course," she said. "That's the Flash I know."

"I don't need any of your cures," I said.

"You've gotten too serious, Flash. I don't like to see you like this."

"And a younger man is going to make me laugh and sing."

"Yes, my dear, trust me."

"OK, Alexandra, go ahead and order him up," I said. "It all sounds very easy."

"He can take your mind off all this," she said. "Brando was always too old for you, anyway."

"Oh, for God's sake, Alexandra, please drop it," I said. "I don't want to be anyone's mother."

"But you already are, my dear. You just don't realize it."

"I don't know what you mean. My husband takes care of himself. Anyway, I don't want to talk about it anymore. I came here to get out of the apartment and rest my worries."

"Your husband," Alexandra said, ignoring me, "made you into his mother so he can go on fighting with her."

"You're an analyst now?"

"Not an analyst, a writer. We're cheaper."

"People aren't that easy to figure out, Alexandra."

"They're not that hard either."

"It's not like in the books," I said.

"That's the typical response of a nonreader," Alexandra said. "What do you know what it's like in books?"

I grimaced. "I hate when you get snotty. I actually read quite a bit."

"You're snotty. The whole lot of you. People think they're so complex and deep, impossible to figure out. In fact, if you read anything at all, you'd see a whole army of hacks have figured you out better than you ever could yourself."

"Maybe so. And the great photographers have already taken your portrait, even if you don't recognize it."

"No comparison, darling. No comparison. A face is a stupid thing, without a life of its own. Character that lies beneath, that is something you can't pick apart with a lens or a mirror. That you have to delve deep for. And few people want to do that."

"My marriage was an ordinary one."

"Pardon me, I disagree. It was complicated, even if in a

fairly ordinary way. Anyone can see it, except for you."

"I suppose you, as the writer looking in, already know more than I do from living out."

"No, but I've known you a while."

I said nothing.

"You don't know it because every life is new to the person living it, but really your story is a very old one: the push and pull. The closeness and then the sudden retreat. Some men, Flash, want to be punished."

"You should write a book about us."

Alexandra smiled. "It's not as easy as I'm making it sound."

"No? I think it's pretty easy. Take one Flash, average-looking woman, icy in her own way. Falls in love with dashing, gorgeous, remote Boy Wonder. He, a master of words; she, involved with the surface of things, with small frozen moments, disconnected story lines."

Alexandra smiled and continued for me: "In a moment of crisis, she meets up with her wild self. But the symmetry is incomplete."

"Because her wild self is just a projection," I put in, "a more glamorous version of her own loser self."

The waiter brought Alexandra's coffee. She took a sip. "In the end," she said, "they both realize they were wrong, but they beat on because that's all they can do, that's all the human being knows, to press on, to defy the void by telling little stories."

"Voilà," I said, smiling. "The plot of your next book."

Alexandra looked at me for a while, studying me. She became serious. Finally she said, "All that's well and good and fun. But I'm through with writing."

"Why?"

Alexandra shrugged. "It's just dumb."

"Dumb? That's your answer?"

Alexandra laughed. "I mean it. Everyone wants you to be an intellectual, but what happens when you're all out of ideas, when you're so exhausted by the world that you can't even form a sentence about it? Except to say dumb. Stupid. Idiotic."

"You're just afraid," I said. "You're afraid of saying what you want."

I expected her to protest, but she looked at me for a moment and then nodded. "Maybe you're right," she said. Then she seemed to reconsider. "But in the end, who cares? In a few days, I'll be off to Baghdad. That's real. I mean, look around, we've made a shit of things. And while the great men were fucking up the world, I was writing little fables. It makes me sick to think about it."

"Come off it, Alexandra, that's just indulgent self-pity. No writer ever saved the world. That's modern narcissism at its worse."

"Now who's the analyst?"

I laughed. I realized, suddenly and to my surprise, that there was something pleasurable in Alexandra's visit. Something long-expected. Or rather a pleasing sort of suffering relief, as when one finally comes down with the flu after dreading it for weeks. Well there, you think. It's done. I have it, and it will soon be over, and I'll be healthy again.

"Yes," I said. "It's pretty easy to figure out other people's lives, isn't it?"

This seemed to stop Alexandra. Something crossed her face, but only for a moment, and she was back to herself. "Yes," she said finally. "You're totally right. No one knows anything about anybody else, isn't that the truth? Other people may even be an illusion, isn't that what they say? We know only our own realities, and dimly at that. Maybe I'm not even sitting across from you, Flash. Maybe I'm an illusion you've projected onto this seat back here, and if you concentrate on something else, *poof!* I'll be gone."

I jumped, and she laughed. "You'll have to concentrate a little harder to get rid of me, though."

After a while she said, "I saw a curious thing in London once." Her voice was very soft now, intimate. She sounded as if she were about to confide something, and I confess that her tone had an odd effect on me. Her voice had always had a soothing, unhurried quality to it. Now, as I listened to another one of her stories, the timbre of her voice made me grateful somehow, made me feel—I can only describe it as—privileged. I was simply happy that she liked me.

"It was late on a Friday night," Alexandra continued. "East End, you know. Friday nights are not like Saturday nights. Fridays are precipice days, the stub ends. For the girl who's been working all week at some shit job, Friday night is the time to slide off into oblivion. Maybe she's a few years over her ideal, putting on weight. She'd imagined it would be like something else, but here she is in the middle of her life, undistinguished in every way. Maybe she stacks cheap underwear at the mall, or sells cosmetics. Every day is just like every other day. Except Friday. Friday she goes out drinking with her girl pals, and for a few hours it's like she has someone else's life. She has a shit boyfriend, too. He's no good, always getting into trouble, disappearing for days. But for a few hours a week, he too is her salvation."

The waiter set down a chocolate brownie in front of us. "On the house," he said. Alexandra gave him a deep smile, one I had seen many times before. But I could see the effect it had on the waiter, who fairly skipped back to his station.

When he was gone, Alexandra broke off a piece of the brownie and chewed slowly. "Well, I saw this girl in London after she'd come out of the pubs. It was late. She was wearing a white summer dress and white high-heeled shoes. She was arguing with her boyfriend. Apparently the argument had been going on for a while, because by the time I came upon them, others had already stopped to look. It was a drunken fight; there was no logic in any of it. They went at it for a while, and then when it seemed everything had calmed, she stepped back and, to my amazement, swung her purse at him, hitting him on the side of his face. He was a little guy, smaller than she was in her heels, with a shaved head. He stood very still for a few moments, didn't even flinch. It was dark, but you can imagine that a red blotch spread from that point on his cheek, right below his left eye. And then he was on her. 'You stupid cunt! You crazy fucking cunt!' His hands were around her throat. A few of the men who had been watching stepped forward then. But before they had to lay any hands on the guy, he had sprung back. I couldn't see his eyes in the darkness, but I remember the streetlight shone off his shaved head. The woman screamed. For a moment it looked as if she were going to hit him again. But then she suddenly turned and ran. The guy stood, stunned. After a moment, he called: 'Molly! Molly! I love you, Molly!' But he didn't move to follow her. She ran back toward the train, her heels clip-clip-clipping and fast. 'Christ, Molly,' the guy said. And then he sat down, right where he was, on the side of the street and put his head in his hands. The others began to walk away. I stood where I was, certain that this fellow had some friends who would come and pick him up and tell him not to worry over the stupid whore. But no one came for him. The crowd broke up. After a few minutes, a group from another pub turned and walked toward him, but it was as if he wasn't there. No one looked twice."

Alexandra stopped. She was watching me as I ate.

I raised my eyebrows.

"You know how this story goes," she said. "Not ten minutes had passed when I heard the sound of white heels on the pavement. Clip, clip, clip. Frantic and fast. Clip, clip. 'Johnny!'"

Alexandra screamed out the name, and the people at the next table stopped and stared.

"They embraced," Alexandra continued, oblivious. "Molly and Johnny, sobbing, both of them—hers shrill and loud and his like something behind glass. 'I love you, Molly,' he said. He had a deep voice. I never forgot that voice. And they stood there for a long time, moving from side to side, and then they walked away from me. I watched them until they turned down a far street. To the end, he had his arm around her shoulder, crushing her to him."

"The human being is a fucked-up creation," I said.

Alexandra smiled, but there was something wounded in the expression. Sitting still now in her black abaya, she almost looked like a penitent or a nun. I don't think she meant to cut me with the story, but when she was done we both sat in silence, embarrassed. When the check came, she insisted on paying. And when she stretched her arm out to get her wallet, I noticed how bony she'd become, and it was my turn to feel sorry for her.

It was late afternoon when we finally walked out of the shop. The heat had lifted, and the fresh air and the breeze invigorated me. Outside now, everything seemed sharp and alive. The plaza was filled with young couples, and when the trolley arrived, bells clanging, it was packed to standing room.

I turned to say good-bye, but Alexandra stopped me.

"Have you been up to the Galata Tower?" she asked.

"I don't think so," I said. "But I've got a lot of work to do, I really should be going."

She took my hand.

"Please, old chap, don't go," she said. "I'm sorry about the story, I didn't mean anything by it."

"Not at all," I said.

"Come, I want to show you something."

I didn't move.

"Please, darling."

"Five minutes, and then I really have to go."

She squeezed my hand—this gesture startled me—and led me down a narrow road that veered steeply out of the plaza down toward the Golden Horn. The pastry and coffee shops immediately gave way to drums and violins and sitars. Some instruments I had never seen. The shops were open to the afternoon breeze, and music drifted out of each of them: a young boy sitting on the floor cradling a blue drum, an old man with young hands beating out a quick song on a tabla, a young woman at a keyboard, the notes high and fragile. We turned down a smaller street where enameled drums in every color hung from the ceiling. Outside a tiny shop, balancing on the stone curb, a man played the clarinet. He nodded as we passed, but continued to play. We hurried down the narrow cobblestone streets, the tower coming in and out of view. Alexandra pointed out stores and landmarks along the way. I followed her down a street full of lights that shone now like jewels in the dusk. "That's the synagogue down that way," she said, pointing with her chin. "And up ahead, of course, there it is: the tower."

It loomed in the dusk. We ran down the street, Alexandra like a bird in her black abaya.

We took the elevator to the top. Again we crowded in, and again Alexandra was oddly silent, her skin tight and lusterless. But up at the top, the wind coming off the Bosporus and the city rising along both sides of it, she seemed to come to life again.

"Breathe," she said, hanging over the railing. "How fabulous, my dear Flash. This is happiness. Everyone thinks the big things will make them happy: if only they were married or had children or got a raise. They forget that those big-ticket dreams have too many moving parts. Let others have the husbands and the kids, my dear. Give me the simplest pleasure, give me the sun setting beyond the Bosporus, standing here next to my good friend Flash, and I'll live happily for a hundred years."

Chapter 15

Istiklal was crowded by the time I left the tower, and the walk home took even longer than usual. It was already dark by the time I opened the garden gate, and I was exhausted. I jumped when I saw the figure under the fig tree, but then he straightened.

The doorman. Had he meant to scare me?

"İyi akşamlar."

"İyi akşamlar." He hesitated.

"What is it?"

He said something in Turkish.

"I'm sorry," I said. "I don't understand."

He spoke some more.

"Repairmen?" I said. "Klima?"

"Evet!" He spoke rapidly and then stopped abruptly. There was something suddenly formal in his bearing. Had I slighted him in some way? Was I treating him like a servant? Or not enough like a servant? What was proper?

"Klima?"

"Klima, evet."

"Bugün?"

"Hayır."

"Tomorrow, then?" I said, using my finger to show the day's turning.

"Evet."

Upstairs, I poured myself a glass of wine and sat on the couch. There were fireworks way up on the Bosporus, and I stayed to watch until they were over and a new set started again farther down the straits.

When it was very late, I went into the room, and seeing the suitcase by the dresser, I dragged it out into the middle of the room and began to unpack. I put everything back in its place, the white socks, the running clothes, the underwear. I folded up the saris, lingering on the cool silk, and put them in the closet. When I was done, I folded up the collapsed suitcase and pushed it under the bed.

That night, I slept the whole night through and woke, late, when my dreams could no longer invent their way around the sounds coming from the apartment upstairs. A desk being dragged across the floor. Something tumbling. A scream.

Chapter 16

Amir Massoud. That was the boy's name.

The convoy had set off from Kandahar at one in the afternoon: the truck carrying the Japanese film crew, a Buick, and our Toyota. I loaded my equipment in the trunk, cushioning it with the suitcases. I wasn't traveling as light as I should have, and it took me a while to make sure all the equipment was secured: seven lenses, three Nikons, the flash, tripod, the bags of film. Photographers now have it so easy. In just a few years, everything shrank. Those bags of film we used to have to carry around, arguing at the X-ray machines, trying to remember if this batch had already passed through once, twice, the bureaucrats at the small broken-down airports refusing to hand-inspect. And then having to pay the AP to transmit anything. Now anyone could travel the war zones of the world with just a camera body or two, a couple lenses, a laptop, and a satellite phone, able to beam a death scene halfway around the world before the blood had even dried. Progress.

It is late summer in southern Afghanistan, the desert rolling out in both directions from the black river of roadway, the convoy making terrific time, the landscape standing still, sand, more sand, and then gentle rises: dunes. In the distance, mountains, maybe, or dust clouds. Now a dark rivulet. A procession of camels, bleached by the sand and sun, knobby-kneed and moving slowly in the heat. The men beside them bent over, swathed in rags, turbans unraveling in the wind. In the distance, mounds of dried sand, homes. People live there, says Alexandra, pointing. Up, up, moving alone on the black road, through the afternoon, the Iranian border just beyond the edge of sand. Shadows and light. After three hours we slow and then stop. Ahead, a small village. Late lunch of watermelons. The two women traveling with the Spaniards go off to find a bathroom. One walks into a cornfield. Shouts from the villagers. Stop, stop, says our driver. Everything not paved over is mined. Death buried everywhere, waiting, unblinking, beneath the living roots of the corn stalks, the fine sand. On my way back to the car, I pass the truck with the Japanese journalists. They are the only ones with air conditioners. But it is their car—they bought it in Quetta. Did they buy the driver also?—ha-ha! Miles making friendly to get a ride. The Japanese journalists haven't gotten out of the car, not even to use the bathroom. They're sitting inside with the windows rolled up and the air conditioner running.

The boy is standing a way off, smoking a cigarette. He watches me pass, taking languid puffs like a pasha. He doesn't move his body, only follows me with his eyes. I stop. "No good," he says to me. "No good." And he beats an imaginary stick across his legs. "Who are you?" I say. "Amir." He is skinny and tall. Up close now I think he might be a few years older than nineteen, but you can't tell with the Afghans. Some boys look like old men by their fifteenth birthday. Amir's face is handsome except for a scar on his chin.

"American womens don't understand," he says. "Very bad what you did."

I ignore him and keep walking. Patrice is outside their car, also smoking. "I don't like that kid," I tell Patrice.

"No, of course you don't." He takes a puff of his cigarette and smiles.

"Looks like a Talib spook," I say.

"Nah," says Patrice. "Taliban? They're not smart enough for any spooking."

I climb back into the car. We have to wait for Amir to finish smoking, and then he joins us in the backseat. The car reeks of cigarettes, and I'm annoyed. Alexandra sits between us, and the boy and I don't exchange another word in her presence. For some reason, and despite my annoyance, this thrills me, as if we already have secrets between us. We drive on, sand, camels, earthen huts. On the side of the road, wrecked Soviet tanks, shredded metal buffed shiny by blowing sand. The tank carcasses casting long shadows in the late afternoon. Bodies filled them once; they rode high in the seats. No cars on the road now, just us in these last three, dropped in from Mars. We stop in the middle of nowhere. Nothing for miles. The cars form an enclosure on the road—

the toilet. First the ladies, then the men. One of the Spaniards in the other car is sick. Arguments. Everyone is hot.
When I bite down, I taste sand. Sand in my hair and eyes.
The arguments go on and on, eternal in the heat, without
resolution. And then we drive on. The shadows longer. After
a while, the men are asleep in the heat, mouths open.

Alexandra turns to me.

"You guys still in Delhi?"

"Yeah, stuck around for the war."

"Up here photographing?"

"All I know how to do," I said.

"Still, tough job in Afghanistan."

"Yeah."

"The living thing issue."

"It's not so bad as long as you don't make it obvious," I
say and shrug.

"Ah, well, radio is easier," she says. "Nothing in the Koran
against disembodied voices."

"Wait for the next edition."

She laughs, open and genuine. We ride in silence, the
light waning.

"It will be dark by the time we get to Herat," she says after
a time. "No good."

"No," I say.

"But it was fun to plan it just so, as if this were that kind
of country."

We ride along, the desert unchanging. She tells me about
Kabul before the war. When she was a little girl, her father
was briefly stationed there for a British agency. Which agency?

I ask. She laughs. "He was a diplomat, I guess." The city was spectacular, full of gardens and fruit; at night the lights sparkled from the hills. "Jewels," she says. Jewels in the hills and in the sky and on the pale lovely necks of the women her parents knew. Elaborate parties thrown on elevated terraces, a garden where water flowed. The house enclosed a courtyard full of pomegranate trees; her brothers used to throw them at one another and play "bleeding."

"Pashto has seven words for the sound a bullet can make," she says. "Did you know that?"

I don't believe her. But she is beautiful and used to having people believe her, so I might as well indulge.

She always wanted to write. But now there's more money in radio or acting as a whore for the foreigners. She laughs at my alarm. Not a real whore, silly. "I'm The Great White Fixer," she says, "the most valuable kind."

She spoke Pashto almost fluently now. Some Farsi. The foreigners trusted her. She understood the country. "The Taliban isn't a problem," she says. "They tolerate me. I know how to cover myself properly." She lived at the old Interconti-nental, and it really wasn't so bad, especially since the bombs had stopped falling.

"And this kid Amir?" I ask in a whisper. She turns to him. His eyes are closed, head resting on the window. She laughs, unsuspicious. "He is the fixer's fixer," she says. "Protection. With benefits."

The shadows lengthen. We stop so the drivers can wash by a stream and pray. When we set off again, I see the lights.

"What's the matter?" Alexandra says.

"Migraine," I say. "You don't have aspirin?"

"Aspirin doesn't help," she says. She takes my left hand. "It will hurt a little, but it will cure the worst of it," she says. And with that she pinches hard into the space between my thumb and forefinger.

I draw back.

"Trust me," she says.

The pain is an electric current. The migraine still lurks, but now it's quieter, waiting just beneath the surface, memory's dull ache.

Chapter 17

Saturday morning, dreaming of sand, I woke before sunrise again. Everything in the room had taken on a damp, wilted feel. The apartment upstairs was silent. Out on the terrace with my coffee, I watched the ships move, listening for the boy selling his wares.

After breakfast, I signed on to check the headlines. Deep in the world section, a small notice about a bomb that had gone off yesterday in Istanbul. No one was hurt. I didn't recognize the neighborhood: I'd never been anywhere near it. The article blamed Kurdish separatists, and some Turkish official promised an immediate crackdown, this will not be tolerated . . . iron fist, blah blah. Just before noon, I tired of waiting for the repairmen and decided to take a walk. The doorman was sitting under the fig tree in the garden, and I waved to him as I closed the gate. "AC repair?" I said. He smiled widely and waved. "İyi günler!" The streets were deserted, everyone hiding from the heat, every blind pulled tight against the glare. "Fine," I said. "İyi günler, then." I began the climb toward Taksim and then changed my mind.

I called Erkan's cell phone. It went to voice mail. I was walking up to the cab stand when he called me back.

"I know it's short notice," I said. "And I'm sorry. I was just wondering if you were free to drive me to the Asian side."

There was a pause.

"Free, yes, it is free."

"No, I'm sorry," I said. "I mean, can you drive me to the Carrefour on the Asian side?"

"I can drive, yes."

"Did I catch you in the middle of something?"

"Middle of what?"

"Never mind, Erkan," I said. "I'm sorry. Can you be here in forty-five minutes? I'm going to go for a tea at the Marmara first."

"Yes, the Marmara. No problem."

I walked the half mile to the Marmara Café. I had not yet sat down when my cell phone rang. I looked out the plate glass windows—the black Mercedes.

"Erkan, you're here already?"

"Yes, I am outside."

The car's windows were tinted, and it was impossible to reconcile the voice on the phone with the car's sudden sinister gleam.

I opened the door and slid into the front seat.

"İyi günler," I said

"Good morning," he said.

He was wearing mirrored sunglasses. The traffic was slow getting past Taksim.

"How long will it take to get to Carrefour?"

"Maybe half an hour, maybe two hours," Erkan said. "Because it is Saturday."

I didn't know what the significance of Saturday was, but I was too tired to try to ask. We sat in silence for a while.

"Erkan," I said as we approached the entrance to the bridge. "Have you ever heard of a photographer named Mira?"

Erkan cocked his head, thinking. "Mira. Family name is?"

I thought back to the letter—had there been a last name?

"I don't remember."

"Mira . . . ," Erkan said. "She work for whom?"

"For whom?" I said. "Sometimes I think you're putting me on with your broken English."

"What, broken?" he said. "Everyone knows—direct object, whom. Easy."

"I'm not sure."

"Yes, sure," he said. "Always For Whom, For Him, For Her."

I laughed. "I mean, Erkan, that I'm not sure for whom . . . for who. I don't know where she works."

We were stopped again, and he looked at me. He raised his eyebrows.

"It's nothing," I said. "I got a letter from her, and I can't for the life of me remember who she is."

"Ah," he said and nodded. "Your life."

He was smiling. Did he misunderstand? Maybe he assumed it had been a friendly letter. Or was he bluffing? The possibility had not occurred to me until he smiled so nonchalantly. Or maybe the beginning of the possibility had dawned on me at the coffee shop when I first looked out at the shiny black Mercedes with its dark windows. A chill went through me. If Erkan's English were better, I might have suspected him. Might it have been him? With a translator? Did he exaggerate his problems with English? But why? Why would he write a letter like that?

"Erkan, do you know any translators?"

"Translators?" he said. "You need document translated, no problem. I do for you."

"Is there an agency?"

"Agency?"

"A place, a business for the translating?"

"Yes, a friend of mine. I say, I do for you."

"Thank you," I said. "I'll let you know."

"What you need translated?" he asked.

I hesitated. "Nothing important."

We made it onto the bridge. Now and then, I looked over at Erkan. He drove with one hand on the wheel, relaxed. Below on the water, the white sails filled and slackened in the wind. The sun reflected off the waves. Silver Water, the name of my neighborhood.

"How about Alexandra Truso?" I said.

"Who?"

"We knew her in India and Afghanistan. She was a radio journalist in Afghanistan, and now she's here, waiting to get into Iraq."

"All of you are crazy, waiting to go to Iraq," Erkan said. "Americans crazy people. Good homes, family, life *çok kolay*, and you want to come here and have bad time."

At the Carrefour I bought some cheeses, cans of lychees, long underwear—all the things I never bought and didn't need but desired only because I couldn't get them anywhere else.

Next door at the home store, I bought two cabinets for the bathroom. The drive back took a long time. Traffic was backed up on the bridge for miles.

"See," said Erkan. "It is Saturday, like I tell you."

All was blue when I returned to my apartment: the water, the hills, the sky. Below stood the Dolmabaçe Palace, surrounded by gardens. And in the distance, the Ortaköy bridge, outlined in lights. The afternoon traffic had picked up, and the cars were lined up in both directions. The sidewalks had begun to fill with people. Below, a white yacht sat docked at the ferry landing. Waiters were moving on the top level, setting up tables, folding napkins. Everything was white—the tablecloths, the flags, the chairs. A quartet was warming up, and as the wind shifted, I could hear Mozart coming in and out of range. In a little while the tables would fill, a space would be made for dancing, a path cut for the bride and groom.

I took out the letter again. I had already worn the paper

smooth, and the sound it made was muted now, as was the effect of the words. It was just a letter, some mad scribblings, a story about someone who wasn't me. I read it through a few times, and then I put it away and poured myself a glass of wine.

I would not run away from the city. This was as much a home as any. Here were my books and my paintings. The rugs we had bought together in Pakistan, in India—Afghanistan. The years spent wearing down distance. Happiness. The hidden courtyards, the secret places, lush in springtime. The bridges and the Bosporus, the Hagia Sophia, Topkapı in the haze, the spires of the Blue Mosque. Wonderboy had been good to me, hadn't he? He'd taught me how to work and love. He understood me. When I had been at my lowest, he had come for me. He'd given me the whole world.

Let us be true to one another. Where nothing lasted, wasn't it up to us to preserve the essential? We were too quick to discard our loyalties now, always yearning for the new, the latest model, the acquisition that would finally bring us freedom. If disappointment could be traded in, effaced, rewritten, then where was the learning? The transcendence that suffering promised and love secured? Where was the desire to prevail, to become better? Promises had to mean something or not be made at all. Till death. Till final parting. To have been true and steadfast to the end. These things still meant something. Ah love, let us be true to one another! The world and its surfeit of pain and petty cruelties; nothing to cling to but tenderness.

❧ ❧ ❧

A crash. The people upstairs at it again. I'm so lonely, I'd whispered. It was before Istanbul; before war, distance, bombs, the letter. Brando perfectly still, his pale eyes unblinking. *Flash, man, life is hard.*

Chapter 18

More than three hours to Herat and night falling. Our convoy moving alone through the dusk, nothing for miles ahead of or behind us. The desert stretching far and wide, the destroyed tanks the only thing to break the monotony of sand. Metal twisted into strange and beautiful shapes. Our driver smoked hashish and played Hindi pop tunes on the cassette deck. Alexandra asleep, Brando and Amir asleep. I rested my head against the window. Those boys with the lizard. I should not have grabbed the stick from them. Once I grabbed the stick, there was no turning back. What had I hoped to teach them anyway? But it wasn't about teaching; it was disgust with them, with me, with the dust and the heat and the despair, the illusion that we knew enough to be better than we were. When I'd taken the stick, it was as if everything that followed had been preordained; I fell into some old order. The poor orphan. So much violence in his small life, and me, a stranger, come out of nowhere to add to it. What had he thought of it all? "Thank you, Mrs. Mister." That's what he said to me when I threw the stick away. That was all: Thank you. Later, when the convoy pulled out, he'd climbed to the top of the compound's walls. As my car passed, he waved good-bye to me, so solemn and old.

The windows were open, and now and then a gust blew the smoke my way. It was sweet and strong. The Hindi music blared, an incongruous sound track to the landscape. You could hear the smiles in the high singing voices. In Kabul, a beautiful former anchorwoman had said to me, "Hopelessness is a sin." Even that final pleasure had been denied her. She had sat in the dark and offered dried fruit and nuts with the tea. She'd helped write a petition to the Taliban, begging that women be allowed to work again. She wanted them to know that the women were not happy with all of the new arrangements. Her husband had grown impatient as she spoke. He'd turned and addressed me. "They're illiterates, you know," he said. "How do you communicate anything to people like that? My dear wife. She's only writing to herself." No one in the West understood it, he said, there was no movement to describe it, but the men were also dying: the beards, the forced piety, the five daily prayers, stifling turbans that needed to be wrapped just so.

All their friends had left. But they refused. They continued to live on the fourth floor with their rugs and silks, and every month another part of the building crumbled away.

I was growing sleepy, but it was an anxious fatigue, and each time I closed my eyes, I felt the bottom sliding away from me. I'd come to Afghanistan and learned there was nothing to hold on to anywhere; the ideas I'd once clung to were made of gossamer. The wind took them. Little girls married to men who could be their grandfathers, widows unable to feed their families, boys like feral cats in the street, stonings, amputations. And then that afternoon at the execution—the horror of it suddenly turned inside out. It was all so ordinary. A jet had roared overhead. The children sold juice and cookies. The Talibs had brought peace, said our driver; this was the cost. Alexandra quoted Leibniz: *All is a plenum.* Everything connects to everything else and exists all at once. "Time is nothing," said Patrice. The heat, the rocking, the smoke. My migraine lurking at the edges. As sleep began to take me, memories bunched together. I imagined a great plane connecting this road to the long shadows to the mud huts to the twisted metal to the individual grains of sand. And then as the edges of my consciousness began to unravel: the sound of wheels on gravel, a sudden stop. All of us instantly awake and alert. The air was sharp. "What the fuck?" Wonderboy's voice. The engine died. Our driver put out his joint. With one fluid, practiced move, he popped out the tape and hid it under the seat. He and Brando got out of the car. There was shouting up ahead. Amir unfolded himself from the backseat without saying anything. Alexandra wrapped her hair and face with her scarf, got out, and ran to follow Brando, the edge of her scarf flapping behind her, silently. I stayed alone in the car, waiting. Within minutes, Wonderboy returned. "The Japs hit someone's goddamn camel."

❧ ❧ ❧

The others surrounded the animal where it lay on the road. The front of the truck was caved in, its windshield cracked. The Japanese crew sat inside, except for one who had joined the discussion around the camel. Amir stood to the side of the car. His fingers were long and brown from the sun. Alexandra had pushed into the crowd and was handling the translations with the two men who must have owned the camel. They were small and thin; they looked like they had been transported from an earlier, sickly age next to the oversize Americans and Europeans. The boy called to me: "American lady." He stood, like someone at a picnic, smoking. Brando stood close to Alexandra. I watched him put a hand on her shoulder and bend in to say something. She turned to him, laughing, her chin turned up. I walked over to the truck. "What happened?" I said to the boy.

Amir shrugged. "The camel, it came to the road. Boom." He watched me for a minute. "You are feeling better now?"

He made some striking motions against his shins and took a drag on his cigarette.

"Yes, I'm feeling better now, thank you."

He smiled. He was pale and lanky, but his face was already mature, his black eyes steady as he spoke to me. He had long lashes. He turned away to blow the smoke.

"It will be expensive now."

"What will be expensive?"

"We must pay. Much money. Maybe the man, he push the camel into the road. Maybe that is only hope."

"That's crazy," I said.

"Crazy for you," he said and spat. When he turned to me again, his face was hard. "That man, he lost everything in wars, now just a few camels, all he can do for his family. But the food for the animal? Not easy. Animal is good and bad, see?"

His English may have been incomplete, but the mockery was eloquent. He gave me a condescending smile.

"Maybe many things impossible for you to know," he continued. "You American ladies, you are like babies, soft and sad. Waaaa! You cry, you laugh, you do what you want. What is easy. This is like childrens do. You get angry and have no control. There is no honor in this life. Afghans—we are poor, but there is honor."

"I fail to see the honor in stoning someone to death."

Amir spat again. "Ah, stoning," he said. "All the Americans are sad about the stonings. Tell me, in America there is no death for criminals?"

"Not for adultery," I said.

He smiled slowly at me. The sun set off gold flecks in his dark eyes. He leaned in closer. He was much taller than me, and I had to look up.

"So adultery is no crime for you?" he said.

"I don't know what you're talking about."

He ran a hand through his curly hair. Was he mocking me?

"I'm talking about honor," he said. His gaze on me was steady.

"I still don't know what you're talking about." But my heart pounded.

After a long moment, he smiled. "That is because you

don't understand the meaning of this word." He spoke with the barely suppressed condescension of someone much older. "Without honor, people cannot live. This man, if he cannot feed his wife and childrens, there is no honor."

"So stone the camel, then."

Amir grinned to show he'd understood the joke. "This is different," he said. "The camel is not thinking or feeling. Men, they pick wrong from thinking and feeling. If someone steals my wife, this man must pay. If no, how do I return to my family? How do I remain a man? So there is stoning. When a cloth tears, you fix it, no? You take needle." He made a sewing motion with his hands and gave me another half smile. "You take the needle and you put the thread inside and then you push in the cloth." His teeth were white and straight. He motioned with his hands, the piercing, all the while looking into my face, the odd mocking tone.

I stood still, rooted to the earth.

He shrugged and opened his palms. "Maybe someday you understand."

Perhaps it was all the time he'd spent among westerners, but Amir lacked the goofy unease with women that seemed so common among young men in Afghanistan then. For years, the only contact men like Amir had with women was with those in their own families—mothers, sisters, aunts. Most emerged stunted and awkward. Amir was different. You wouldn't know it by the way he talked, but something foreign had crept into his way of being. For all his grasping toward tradition, Amir did not seem wholly at home in his own country. With me, he'd adopted a loose familiarity that

I could have mistaken for disrespect. Except that at times it seemed genuine in spite of his mockery, as if something had escaped him. He moved slowly, took his time when he spoke.

"How old are you?" I said.

Amir shrugged. "Nineteen years, twenty. How old are you?"

"Almost thirty."

"Then I am almost thirty also," he said.

"Where are your mother and father?" I asked.

"Father is dead, mother is no more."

He flicked the cigarette away. The sky was cloudless and had begun to turn pink where it met the horizon. One of the drivers had taken his prayer rug out to a small stream and was kneeling in the sand.

With one fluid move, Amir pushed away from the car.

The crowd parted and grew silent. Wonderboy stood close to Alexandra. The two Afghans stood off to the side, discussing something. I walked to the middle of the road. There was a moaning sound from near the ground. I stepped closer. The camel was still alive. He lay with his head bent awkwardly, his eyes open wide. As I watched, he kicked suddenly, a furious scramble with his front leg. I took a step back. The camel let out another low moan, one eye turned, it seemed, toward me. The animal's body stank of sweat and struggle. The Afghans returned, pointing to the dying camel and shouting. Already, the Japanese man was counting out his dollars. And then he stopped suddenly. Some new disagreement? Alexandra, translating: "He says it was all they had. One hundred, that is the minimum."

And then Amir walked to where the camel lay. The animal stopped moving. He was expecting him. Everything was as it had to be, nothing was out of place. Amir reached into the pocket of his *shalwar*. The pistol was black and heavy. Nothing shone on it. I jumped back. He aimed and fired two shots into the animal's head. The neck snapped back. I covered my face with my hands. The sound of the gunshots echoed off the hills. And then more shouting as the others came running.

It is a good sound, American lady. The suffering is finished.

Chapter 19

Late August. I wandered Istanbul for hours, like someone looking for a lost object. I visited the sights, searching beneath every stone, willing myself to remember. I would be gone soon. I bought fruit from the street vendors. Climbed to the top of the old fort.

On Saturday night, I went to a concert at Harbiye. I hid a Brie and smoked salmon sandwich in my backpack and filled a water bottle with vodka. It was a clear night, and though the day had been hot, the night was cool. All the stars were out; someone with patience and dedication might have counted to the last one.

After, I walked back to my apartment contentedly, slowly. The entire city was awake. Couples, old women, young men in a hurry. Even the drab alleys were colored with summer. Red cherries for sale in the wooden carts; an orange bag full of plums; the purple flowers behind the barricades at the Japanese consulate. And from every side street, the Bosporus sneaking in, surging, serenely lovely, and silvered with moonlight.

At the apartment I took the stairs two at a time. I decided then—I'd never been more sure of anything—that I would remain in Istanbul. I was as at home here as I was anywhere. The city's rhythms had become mine: the fruit that appeared seasonally (strawberries, green plums, soon the green and purple figs), the boy's calling in the dark, the five daily prayers. This is what it meant to be part of a place, knowing how the hours stacked up, understanding the multitude of small things that made up the day. I had been in Istanbul long enough now that I knew it intimately, knew the way the city expanded and contracted with the seasons, how the sidewalks filled, emptied, and filled again, the turning of leaves, the stadium that roared and shook to life on the weekends. And running through its spine, the Bosporus, the theme of Istanbul. Calm, tumultuous, beautiful, terrifying, but steady and deep.

When you first get to a city, all of it is mystery. Then little by little you learn the streets and find the shortcuts, the quiet alleys. You learn which avenues connect, which are dead ends. After a while you begin to get a picture in your mind of what the city looks like; you could walk it blindfolded. In this way, little by little, you trade mystery for comfort. After a while, you imagine you know a place

The door was unlocked. "Brando?"

For a moment, my heart leapt and I forgot everything, the tears and the anger, the ordinary betrayals. Wonderboy had come home! But then I heard Turkish and the doorman's voice.

The air-conditioning guys? At this hour? I put my things down and walked to the back. My bed had been pushed to the side of the room, against the wall. And the two repairmen stood in the middle, parts from the disassembled unit between them. The doorman sat on the windowsill, watching. Next to him, wearing her black abaya, sat Alexandra. It took me a few moments to recognize her. I was so focused on the destruction of my air conditioner, now reduced to a hundred pieces on my bedroom floor, that I had not noticed her at first. But there she was, undeniably herself, sitting in my bedroom and having an animated conversation with the doorman as if they had known each other for years.

I took a step forward. The dismembered air conditioner stood between us.

"What's going on?"

She smiled first at me and then at the doorman. "I'm helping with your air conditioner," she said. "It's a mess."

"Who let you up?" I was careful not to sound confrontational.

She glanced at the doorman.

"Didn't you tell Bashir that he could let the repairmen up?" she said.

"The repairmen, yes. But I didn't know you were in the neighborhood."

"Me?" she said. "I had come by to say hello, and Bashir was there with the klima guys. I think at first he mistook me for you. Where have you been?"

I laughed. "You're my mother now?"

"It's just that it's late," she said. "You shouldn't be out walking by yourself. It's not exactly safe."

"I'm fine," I said.

"Well, it's really not safe."

"Alexandra, the scariest thing that happened to me tonight was walking into my apartment at ten o'clock and finding my air conditioner in pieces and strangers in my house."

"My dear," she said. "Surely you must be used to all this by now."

I sighed. "I'm tired," I said.

"Go, darling," said Alexandra, shooing me. "Pour yourself a glass of wine and relax. I'll take care of these guys for you."

"Thanks," I said. "Some wine would be good."

The doorman said something to Alexandra, and she turned to me. "Bashir wants to know if he can leave."

"Of course," I said.

He bowed to me on his way out. When he was gone, Alexandra said, "Do you know where he lives?"

"What are you talking about? The doorman?"

"In a little closet. There isn't even a proper window."

"He doesn't live-live in there, though."

"Yes, he does," she said. "He's got a little bedroll and a low table."

"Oh," I said.

"You didn't know that, did you?"

"Oh, come on, Alexandra," I said. "I'm just a photographer, not freakin' Mother Teresa."

"Do you ever get involved in anything at all?"

"Not in other people's living arrangements, no." I said. I must have sounded angry, because Alexandra looked away.

"Look," I said. "I'm tired and would like to go to sleep. Can you find out how long this is going to take? I'll get you some wine."

Alexandra took a small, ironic bow. But the old hardness had returned to her eyes.

I went into the kitchen and poured Alexandra a glass of Gamay. I stood for a moment at the threshold, listening to the conversation between her and the repairmen, and walked back to the bedroom.

"Looks like the filter clogged and the unit froze," Alexandra said, taking the wine. "But they're checking the compressor just to be sure."

"When are they going to finish?"

"Maybe tonight, maybe tomorrow."

"Tonight is impossible," I said. "I need to go to bed. Can you tell them to come back in the morning?"

Alexandra watched me for a moment. Then she bent from the waist. "Yes, great *pasha-bayan*, anything you say. At your service."

I grimaced, and she turned away from me.

She exchanged a few words with the klima guys.

"Tomorrow at nine a.m. good for you?"

"Sure," I said. "Especially since I know they won't show up."

❧   ❧   ❧

Back in the kitchen, I poured myself a glass of wine and took it out into the balcony. After a few minutes, Alexandra joined me. I heard the sliding door open and then close.

"I was out walking," she said. "I didn't expect to come by here. But I passed by and saw the light on."

"I was at a concert."

"By yourself."

"It's how I've been doing just about everything for the last couple of years."

Alexandra was quiet.

"I know I sound like a self-pitying jerk," I said. "Up here in this mansion, wanting for nothing, the world at my feet, but still complaining."

"Nah," Alexandra said. "Self-pitying maybe, but not a jerk."

"Maybe you're right. What I need is a younger man."

I felt Alexandra stiffen. "Don't listen to me," she said. "I'm as full of shit as anyone else."

Something was troubling Alexandra. I had sensed it since the first day, and now it was more pronounced.

"Why were you walking around late if it's so dangerous out?"

"I have an excuse," Alexandra said.

"Oh?"

"Claustrophobia."

"You're kidding."

"I'm not," she said. "It's much better now, but every once in a while, I need to get out or I'll choke."

"Have you always had it?" I was skeptical.

"Started a few years ago," she said. "You know I was in Kandahar on September 11?"

"Is that so?" I said.

"My concern that day was to get up to the north, where Massoud had been attacked."

I took a sharp breath and then caught myself. But Alexandra had already noticed. She looked down at me.

"Ahmed Shah, I mean," she said. "I suspected he had died instantly, but still I wanted to go and see for myself. I had arranged for a UN flight the next day when I got a call late that afternoon telling me that they were canceling because of what had happened in New York. I eventually made it up there and ended up covering the invasion, working for radio during the day and translating in the afternoons. I got to Kabul just ahead of the Americans."

She looked at me, seemed to make a decision, and then continued. "I ran into Brando there at the Intercon. You had already left for Miami, I think."

I nodded. Alexandra and Brando at the Intercontinental. Why would she tell me that?

"Anyway, you've heard the stories, I'm sure," she said. "Kabul was a total blast. It was like earthquake, revolution, and jailbreak all at once. No one understood what the fuck was going on, except that there was this sense of release. Remember when we were there in '98? The empty streets? Nothing like that now. Nothing. I don't remember the Afghans ever being that exuberant."

"I was there after the invasion," I said.

"Right. Anyway," Alexandra continued. "Now and then when I was out reporting I would feel out of breath. But I attributed it to all the excitement and lack of sleep. I didn't really think much of it. Then I flew back to the States before Christmas, and as soon as they closed the doors to the airplane, I was overcome with a hot, closed panic. I thought: I am trapped now inside this metal container, and for the next ten hours I cannot leave it. I didn't recognize it as claustrophobia at the time, it seemed something far more personal, a kind of private crisis. I spent the rest of the flight trying to breathe deeply and meditate. The sweat poured off me. When we finally landed at JFK and they opened the door to the jetway, I felt the air rush in, felt it as if it were a person, a living thing, bright, vital. In the cab on the way in, I lowered the windows and inhaled that cold sharp air. I was wildly happy, unreasonably so, and I knew that it was all part of some pathology, but I didn't want to think about it too deeply because I was just glad to be out, away from enclosures."

She took a sip of wine and then a deep breath.

"I was good for a while after that, and then one day, I took a cab up Fifth Avenue. The car stopped around Twenty-third, and the traffic closed in on us. We couldn't move for several long minutes, and then the horn-honking started. I was suddenly overcome by the same feeling, sharper this time. I could see out, look at people walking, people waiting by the sidewalk, and I couldn't believe that they were not suffering too. The sense of enclosure was so total that I imagined it took in the entire world. I paid quickly and left the cab.

"But that release was not as complete as the first one. The street was crowded and it was like emerging, not into freedom, but into an only slightly larger space. I walked quickly, knowing that if I gave into my panic, I would never make it home. Back in the apartment, the terror subsided. I slept with the windows open, and the next morning I woke with the sun in my eyes. The world had been set right overnight, as sometimes happens. And I was OK for a few days, though by now I had come to know the suffocating closeness of things and could not be completely at ease.

"So it went for some weeks, the source of the claustrophobia more intimate each time it struck again: elevators, bathrooms, someone's breath on me in the subway. I could not work. That February, I traveled to Boston to see some friends. In the train I closed my eyes. By then I had perfected a certain passivity in the face of it, and I learned that by not fighting it too much, I could endure the sense of confinement, even take a certain horrified pleasure in it. There was a dinner. Some friends, radio people. The same stories, the same arguments. You know how it is. Fleeing the kitchen, I stood out in the middle of the yard. It was freezing, and I knew the others would think I'd gone mad. But I could not stand to be in that kitchen. I wanted to be away from the smells, the sounds, the presence, of others. And then at once, I became aware of something that I could only describe as a second world behind this one. I understood something very basic, something mystics have known all along, but that for the first time I understood in a way that was without thinking. But it wasn't any kind of happy revelation, you know. Nothing with angels singing or shit like that. No, instead, this feeling struck me as the ultimate claustrophobia, as if all my panic had been leading me to this one truth: that the world that I inhabited was nothing more than what I could know through my senses and that they told me nothing of the reality outside our mind, nothing of the space beyond what we could smell or hear or touch. I felt, I don't know how to describe this to you, Flash, I felt trapped inside myself, but not myself as an individual. What I mean is, I felt trapped inside my humanness, felt the limitations of our biology press down on me like four walls. I had the feeling that if I stopped breathing I might break through to that other side I knew existed beyond sense, but it was like being unable to wake from a dream. And then there was this immense sadness that came from sensing what it all meant, not even really understanding it, just somehow feeling that all I would ever think of as real would never extend beyond sight, touch, sound."

I was staring at her.

Alexandra's face had been serious and distracted as she told me the story. Seeing me must have chastened her, because she continued now, a little more reserved.

"I stayed in bed for three days after that," she said. "Everyone thought I had the flu and treated me with the kind of gentleness rarely accorded the healthy."

Alexandra was quiet for a moment, and then she looked away. "It's funny, isn't it? How everything shifts when we see someone suffer. That old notion of sorrow to cleanse your sins . . ."

She stopped. "At any rate, the experience cured me of the claustrophobia for a time," she said. "But I knew when it returned, it would be more terrible still. I imagined it becoming a permanent condition, becoming like one of those people who suffer from constant vertigo. So I'm careful to avoid tight spaces, and when I feel that panic start, like a closing of the throat, I get out. A fast walk, even an escape to a balcony where I can feel the wind in my face."

"You still fly?" I said.

"Short distances, yes," she said. "Actually planes are not so bad as cars, especially in traffic jams. It's why I prefer to walk."

"That sense of enclosure," I began. "I suppose we've all felt it, one way or another."

"Yes," Alexandra said. "I suppose. Though I don't think we really ever know where it comes from."

There was a good breeze on the balcony, and Alexandra seemed at ease. I watched her as she spoke, her face turned out toward the water, watching the other shore.

After Alexandra left, I locked the door and poured myself the rest of the bottle. I sat on the couch and took out the letter again. I thought of what Alexandra had said, and how, in its own strange way, the letter had ushered me into a kind of claustrophobic waiting.

I closed my eyes, but couldn't sleep. Something gnawed at me. What was it? The Japanese had called for the third time about the tombs project, and I had put them off again.

Soon I would have to return the money. But it wasn't that. My still-pending visa? I needed to take care of the travel arrangements. Yes, maybe it was that. Before the letter, I had been calling every week to get an update on my papers. I had neglected my work. But was it my work or Brando's? Whose idea was all this travel? I stood and walked out on the balcony. The pigeons circled and dove around the illuminated minarets of the Dolmabaçe Mosque. Far down the Bosporus, a few late fireworks exploded soundlessly. It was a clear, cool night of hard edges. Topkapı was all straight lines and solid history at the mouth of the Bosporus. Behind it, the dome of the Hagia Sophia. Istanbul didn't exist on one plane—it was a city of layers. Every monument hid a secret past: the mosque that was a church, the restaurant that was a brothel. In the Hagia Sophia, restorers were still finding Byzantine mosaics under layers of plaster. No one could tell how much had been painted over, effaced, forgotten. Thousands of pages of Ottoman records lay disintegrating in storage, their script unreadable now, so many stories lost in the translation from one way of life into another.

I returned to the couch and lay down. The ringing phone woke me when it was still dark.

"Tunes."

"Hey."

"Awful day."

"Yeah, here too," I said.

"What do you mean, there too?"

"Nothing," I said.

"Why are you still in Istanbul?"

"Because I'm not attached to a giant multinational media empire."

"Tunes, man, no need to be nasty."

"You know, I'm really sick of this," I said.

"Sick of what?"

"All of this, this bullshit life."

"What are you talking about, bullshit life? You live like royalty. You want a bullshit life, man, come to Iraq."

"The AC guys were here tonight. You know what time? Ten p.m. They hadn't showered in a month. I'm not going to be able to sleep in that room again."

"So it's fixed."

"What's fixed?"

"The AC, it's fixed?"

"No, it's not fixed," I said. "It's in pieces on the bedroom floor."

I began to cry.

"Tunes, man, what's wrong with you? It's just an AC. Get some perspective."

"Don't tell me to get perspective, Brando," I said. "You don't know anything."

"Snap out of it, Tunes," he said, angry now. "I just interviewed the family of a three-year-old who was killed by a sniper. That's real life."

I wiped my nose.

"Snipers: We bring meaning to your life," I said. "They should wear it on their T-shirts."

"I'm glad you can laugh about it."

"You hear me laughing?"

"Life is hard, man. You should have seen this mother; she just sat, stunned, not crying, not screaming. The little boy had been playing in the street. The blood was still on the front steps when I got there."

"Oh, shut up," I said. "Just shut up."

No, my marriage had not been happy. Is anyone's? Everyone thought ours was. But it was just an ordinary marriage, the kind where happiness doesn't even enter into the reckoning. When you first meet, your love is a stranger. Years go by—you are bound together through moves, new cities, shared friends. You travel. You wake up and make love, you go out for dinner, you do the laundry. Beneath the surface of things, everything is changing except the one: the stranger you married is still the person you don't know.

Wonderboy could lie so easily. Not about the big things—I never caught him at those. But the small things, the things that didn't even matter.

That time friends of his had invited us to dinner. Wonderboy had to work late again. He told me to go ahead, that he had just talked to them and they were waiting for me. "Charlie says they only invite us to see you anyway," Wonderboy said.

Except that when I arrived, no one was home. We had the date wrong. The party had been scheduled for the following evening, when Charlie and his wife would be getting in from Atlanta. Wonderboy had never even talked to them. He could lie so easily about so little.

The blood was still on the front steps when I got there. Had it moved Wonderboy to a place deeper than outrage?

Chapter 20

The repairmen, of course, did not show up the following morning. Just after noon, the downstairs bell finally rang. I buzzed the door open. But the person who came up the stairs was Alexandra.

"No-shows, huh?"

"Told you."

"Well, it's too beautiful a day to mope around up here," Alexandra said. She paced up and down the great room, the black abaya flapping behind her. "You need to snap out of this thing, Flash, you need to get back to work. Forget about Brando."

"I'd like to."

She walked to the window and turned around, animated.

"I know!" she said and turned again to point out to the middle of the Bosporus. "Let's go there! Bring your camera."

"Go where?"

"There, that island there."

"I'm not interested," I said. "And, anyway, I have no desire to shoot."

"Come on, Flash," she said. "Fine, leave your camera. But let's go see the tower. The view is wonderful—I went there with my Turkish classes."

"You go to Turkish classes?"

"How do you live here without speaking Turkish?"

"I speak a little," I said, defensive now. "I have a note-book."

She waved me away. "We can get a *vapeur* to take us there. It's easy."

It wasn't all that easy. Alexandra may have been proud of her Turkish, but once we got down to the docks, no one could understand it. I shouldn't be catty. My notebook was of even less help. "You're very kind" and "I'm so dumb" only goes so far when you need something concrete. We ended up walking a few blocks down to Beşiktaş —Alexandra refused to board a bus—to wait for a ferry that would to take us to the Asian side. From there, Alexandra was certain, we could find a small motorboat to take us to the tower.

It was a warm day, the sun still out. The sky was clear, and as we pulled away from the shore, I could not help but gasp at the sight of the city we left behind, everything awash in blues and grays, Topkapı grand on its promontory, the stacked homes neat in the distance, windows catching the light.

"It's so gorgeous," I murmured.

"It is," Alexandra said. "I really never tire of this city."

We sat in silence for a little while, the ferry parting the water, the sound of the motor, the smell of fuel, the diving birds. A boy came down the deck, and Alexandra and I pulled our legs in to let him pass.

"Have you ever really looked at the faces of commuters?" Alexandra said. "Doesn't matter how gorgeous the city is, they all look like they're going home to die."

It was just after five, and the ferry was packed. Young people and women had spilled to the outside deck. Inside sat the salarymen, staring ahead.

"Life—a genuine life—is about fighting the dulling influence of adaptation," Alexandra said.

I turned away from the men and stared at Alexandra. "I don't have the slightest idea what you're talking about," I said.

"I'm saying that with time, we become inured to pain," Alexandra said. "But also to beauty."

I thought for a moment. "It's like the Turkish Gamay," I said.

"What?"

"The awful wine here," I said. "You get used to that, too."

Alexandra laughed.

"But you know, I'm glad for it," I said.

"I'm sure," Alexandra said. "It's what kept you in a bad marriage all those years."

I didn't respond.

"I'm sorry," she said. "I overstepped."

"Well," I said, "I suppose I got used to the beautiful parts too."

❧ ❧ ❧

We disembarked on the Asian shore just as another ferry was pulling out.

"Hurry," Alexandra said, taking my hand. The business-men walked quickly to the waiting buses. We dodged them, racing along the seawall. Families were out for a stroll, and all along the water's edge men grilled little fish and green peppers on portable stoves.

Alexandra pulled me along, and I struggled to keep up. By the time we reached the dock opposite the tower, I was panting, though Alexandra was not even sweating.

"Where are the damn boats?" Alexandra said. I stood watching as she walked up to a couple canoodling on the wall. She returned, rolling her eyes.

"They look at me like I'm mad," she said. "I know there are boats. I just took one. Have you ever been up there?"

I shook my head. I was still out of breath and felt light-headed, though part of it may have been the disorientation of seeing my apartment building from this other shore, as if I were gazing back at myself through a mirror. This is the far shore, I thought. Here I am, the place where the lights shift and dim every night.

"It's a small little spit of land and the restaurant is terri-ble," Alexandra said. "But the view is good. And the story is better."

"The story of what."

"The tower—Maiden's Tower, that's what Kız Kulesi means."

"I thought you said there were boats."

"There are boats. There were boats. We'll find them."

I stood around for a few more minutes as Alexandra left to ask more people about the boats that had not materialized. After a few minutes, I sat on the wall to wait. She finally returned and shook her head.

"Sorry, Flash. I led you on a pointless journey," she said. "I don't know where the boats are."

She sat next to me, and we stared out over the water at the tower in silence. After a moment, she jumped up.

"I'm hungry," she said. "Let me buy you dinner, and maybe you'll forgive me."

We walked back along the seawall. Alexandra bought us two fish sandwiches from the grillers near the docks, and we ate them as we waited for the return ferry. It was almost dark now, and cool. In the ferry, we sat inside, on the side facing the tower.

"There was this king and this queen," Alexandra said, and it took me a moment to understand she was about to tell me a story, though I should have been damned well used to it by then. I suspected this was the point of the trip after all. Not to see the tower, but to talk about it.

"They desperately wanted a child, but year after year, they failed. So finally one year, the king gathered all the magicians in the land and begged them to do something."

Alexandra looked out the window as she spoke. The European shore grew.

"What would infertile women do without magicians?" I said.

"This is a serious story, Flash," Alexandra said. "May I finish?"

I nodded.

"So he gathers all the magicians together. They do their thing, the king and queen do their thing. And voilà, nine months later, a beautiful daughter is born to the royal couple. The king, overjoyed, called all the magicians back for a wondrous festival. But one of the invitations got lost in the mail."

"That happens," I said. "Should have sent it FedEx."

Alexandra smiled. "Anyway, one of the magicians didn't get his invite, and he was super pissed. So he shows up at the tail end of the festivities and puts a horrible curse on the king. Tells him that he himself will be the agent of his daughter's death before she turns eighteen."

"Very ungracious," I said. "You'd think the wise would be better than the rest of us."

"They're not, my dear. This magician was a real badass. So what does the king do? He banishes his daughter to the tower, to live alone. For her own good, of course. Me, I think the king was old-school: you know, 'Leave it to me, you stupid woman—I'll handle everything.' So for seventeen years, the girl lived alone in the high lovely tower, enduring an exile that, whatever its loneliness, promised a long life and great happiness in the end."

"Oh, no," I said. "I don't want to hear this story."

"The day before the princess was to turn eighteen," Alexandra continued, "her father prepared a magnificent basket overflowing with fruits and sweets. He secured his finest servant to deliver it. But as the basket stood overnight outside the servant's door, unbeknownst to anyone, a serpent entered and coiled within. The following morning, the basket was delivered. The girl cried with joy. And when she set aside the silken cloth, the sleeping serpent woke."

"I hate these kinds of stories," I said.

"That's the story of the Maiden's Tower," she said. "I didn't make it up. Though I'll admit the blank verse is all mine."

We decided to walk from Beşiktaş to my apartment. The night was beautiful, and the young people were out, laughing and jostling one another. When we began the climb to my street, I turned to Alexandra.

"Did you ever want children?"

"Oh God, no," she said cheerfully. "Never. You forget I raised four younger brothers practically on my own. My father was too important to ever be around, and my mother was too busy being thin. I got that whole child thing out of my system early."

I was quiet.

"You?" she said.

"I didn't think so," I said. "But now I'm not so sure."

Alexandra shrugged. "Children aren't all that great to have around. Trust me."

❊   ❊   ❊

That night, I wrote Brando an e-mail. Call me, please. I need to talk to you. Then I took a glass of wine out to the living room and sat facing the water. The Maiden's Tower shone in the dark, a small lighthouse, blinking.

Chapter 21

We had arrived in Herat late in the afternoon. We'd been shown to our rooms, washed, eaten a quick meal of melons, and then night had fallen quickly, more quickly than anywhere else in the world. One minute the world was on fire, and the next it was extinguished. They kept a candle burning on a shelf in the hallway, but once you closed the door, the light was just a faint flicker beneath the door. There were no curtains on the windows, but the night was black and moonless. I undressed in the dark. Wonderboy was already in bed. "It's been a long day," he said.

I pulled myself up. "Yes," I said. I touched his face. He remained still. His skin was tight and cool.

"You cried when they shot the camel," I said.

He was quiet for a long while, but I could hear his breathing.

"It was sad," he said at last. "You saw how he moved his legs."

I didn't say anything. Wonderboy's face was in shadows; I could make out only the bulk of his body in the darkness.

"Like he was asking for help," he said. "I know that's not

how you're supposed to see things, but that's what it looked like."

"At the execution," I said, "you only took notes."

Wonderboy shifted beneath the sheets. We were both quiet. After a moment, he reached for me, took my hand, and pressed it to his lips. But before I could react, he drew it away.

"Animals are innocent," he said. "People are always guilty of something."

Chapter 22

Just before dawn, my cell phone woke me. I stood from the couch and began to search for it. When I finally remembered it was in my purse, the ringing had stopped. I checked the call log. Brando. I lay back on the couch, but couldn't sleep. The speakers went on in the mosque and I braced myself for the call to prayer. *Allahu Akbar, Allahu Akbar. Ash hadu al-la llaha ill Allah . . .* I had memorized most of the prayer without trying. When it was over, I sat where I was to watch the dawn come up, and then I made myself some coffee. When the sun was brightening the sky, the phone rang again, and I ran to get it.

"Tunes."

"What's going on?"

"My God, Tunes."

"Are you all right?"

"I'm fine. I got your message. I'm sorry I haven't called. I was on patrol."

"On patrol?"

"Embed, Sunni triangle. Tunes, you can't believe what's going on out here."

"I'm glad you're OK," I said. "I wanted to talk to you about something."

"I'm fine, I'm OK . . . Oh God, Tunes."

I hesitated. "What happened?" I finally said. "What's the matter?"

"How are you, Tunes?"

"It's early. First tell me what's wrong. Are you all right?"

"I'm OK. Don't worry. I'm fine."

"What's going on? Where are you?"

"It wasn't my idea. Just awful. Young guy. Wasn't my idea to go back. Sidney, he wanted the shot. Someone else had the shot. He wanted the shot."

"What shot?"

"The shot from the top."

"The photo, you mean? Or was Sidney shot?"

"No, no. I'm fine. Don't worry. Sidney's fine. But the kid, God, Tunes, the kid was eighteen. From some no-name city in bum-fuck God-knows-fucking-where. It hadn't been my idea, I stayed behind. And goddamn it if there weren't still bad guys up there. Motherfuckers. Ah, Tunes. Tunes, it's awful. Like the end of the world here."

"Are you OK? I don't understand what you're saying. What happened? Where are you calling from now?"

"Tunes, man. I love you so much. Please don't leave me, you hear? Please don't. I would die without you. I mean it. I can't live without you. I love you so much. I wouldn't be able to go on without you."

"Don't talk like that."

"I mean it. All of this. This is such fucking bullshit. I love you. I've loved you since that first day when we saw the sun set over the Everglades."

"When was the last time you slept?"

"Goddamn it, Tunes! People are dying, and you're asking me about sleep?"

"You are delirious, Brando. I can't talk to you like this."

"Delirious? You're the one who is delirious. I'm here spilling my guts to you, telling you I almost died tonight, and all you can do is criticize me."

"Criticize?"

"I wish for once in your life you would listen to yourself. I mean, it's astonishing. I wish that I could just say something that wouldn't incur your automatic wrath. What is it that I need to do?"

"For God's sake, Brando, what are you talking about?"

"Your contempt for me is manifest in every word that you utter. The only thing I am sure of when I tell you something is that I am going to get a sneering, contemptuous response, which denounces my opinions as idiotic and narcissistic."

"You're tired and lashing out at me for no reason, Brando. Just stop it."

"Look, I know I've been a dick; that doesn't give you the right to just treat me like shit. I have feelings too. I'm a human being too. I almost died tonight. Tunes, it's the end of the world here. You have no idea. No one gives a shit about this place."

"Brando, please stop. You're tired. That's all, you're just tired. Are you sure you're OK? Were you hit?"

"Come on, Tunes."

"You weren't hit? You're OK?"

"Oh my God. Hit or not hit, what's the difference? You have no idea what it's like out here."

I was quiet for a long time. The static on the line grew and then flattened.

"Look, I'm fine," Wonderboy finally said, his voice calmer now, almost intimate, the old voice. "I'm sorry I said that about you not knowing what it's like. I, ah—I'm sorry. We've been through a lot together, Tunes. I didn't mean to . . . Well, you know that I didn't mean to. You've done all right, you know. I know it's been hard for you. War is hell, and you know I'm not proud of everything either. And it was—"

"You're tired," I said. "You need to sleep. Just sleep, Brando."

The line went dead. A few minutes later, the phone rang again.

"You know, Tunes, I call you, I talk to you, and it's like you don't even care if I call or not, like you can't be bothered."

"What the hell are you talking about? You don't know shit about me."

"I'm talking about that, your voice. It's flat, like you don't care if I live or die."

"Spare me the dramatics, will you, Mr. War Hero?"

"Listen to you, your anger is just dripping. You don't want me to call you anymore, I won't call you anymore. There's a war going on, Tunes. It may not mean anything to you anymore, but people are dying."

"And you're going to save everyone by writing about it."

"Your contempt and your sarcasm are unbelievable. It's like I don't know you anymore. I'm busting my butt out here, Tunes. And where are you? We used to be a team. How long are you going to stay away? This is life and death out here."

"It's life and death everywhere."

"You know what, you don't want me to call you anymore, I won't call you anymore."

"Do what you want."

There was another long pause.

"Tunes, man, we used to be a team, and—"

"Is someone staying in your room with you?" I said. "Is that what it is?"

"What the hell are you talking about?"

"I'm talking about why you keep calling me from the roof," I said. "I'm talking about Nadia or whatever the fuck her name is."

"What?"

"What? That's all you can say. Answer me, Brando, is someone staying in your room?"

"It's like you've lost your mind," he said. "I have no fucking idea what you're talking about. Nadia? What the hell are you saying? What are you accusing me of? I almost fucking died tonight, and you're—I don't even know what you're doing."

"Fuck you."

❧ ❧ ❧

A few minutes later the phone rang. It rang several more times until I turned it off.

As if they'd been waiting for me to hang up, the people upstairs started fighting again.

"Shut up!" I shouted up to the ceiling. "Shut the fuck up!"

The racket continued. My head was on fire. I didn't know what I wanted, what I thought, what was going on. Shut up! I went to my office and tore through my drawers. When I'd found a pen and paper, I leaned over and tried to steady my hands. Within minutes, I'd written a quick and angry note.

Dear Honeymooners:
For almost a year, I have listened to your pointless arguments, endured the scraping of furniture, winced at the sound of breaking glass. That you are still alive is a wonder, a happy one for yourselves and a less happy one for me. Will you please, please, please, please SHUT UP.

I underlined SHUT UP three times. I knew it made me seem like a nut. Fine, I was a nut. I'd been driven to it by these two strangers, whom I'd never met, whom I knew only by the scrape and whine of their voices. These giants who shouted and swung from the ceiling, who could move heavy furniture with one finger back and forth across the parquet floors, charged with the superhuman strength of their mutual hatred.

I folded the note and, with little thought to consequence, ran up the stairs and pounded on the door. The shouting stopped. I pounded again.

"Hello."

Not a sound from the apartment. But the peephole darkened briefly.

"Please have some consideration," I shouted.

Light flowed through the hole again.

I knocked one more time, then slipped the note beneath the door.

I raced back down to my apartment, my heart pounding. I poured myself a glass of Gamay. Goddamn Brando and all his stupid boy obsessions. Goddamn this pointless war and all the fixers and con artists and killers that have flocked to it.

Chapter 23

I lay awake beside Brando in a narrow bed at the old UN guesthouse. In the hallway, a small candle burned on a shelf, the only light. I stood for a moment, listening. The others locked away in their own rooms, the entire guesthouse asleep. In the bathroom, another candle burned in the tub, but it was not enough to mask the smell. The floor sticky beneath my bare feet. I squatted over the toilet, careful not to touch anything. On the way back, I passed Alexandra's room. She and Amir were locked in their own world, like the others. I stopped in front of the closed door. I shifted my weight, and a floorboard groaned. After a moment, I heard noises, the rhythmic creaking of the old bedsprings. Then a whisper, a small cry, her voice first and then his, murmuring, guiding. I returned to our room, feeling my way back to bed. The days had been warm, but the night was chilled, and I moved close to my husband to calm the shivers. He shifted away in sleep. The next room was quiet again, and I returned alone to the night silence, the penetrating darkness of Afghanistan.

The next morning, I watched Brando dress.

"They're going to get us all in trouble," I said.

"Who?"

"Alexandra and her boy lover."

"It's none of my business what she does."

"None of mine either," I said. "I could care less. But we're time travelers in the year 1425. It can't end well."

"They're discreet," Brando said. "Don't worry about it."

"I don't like it," I said.

Brando pulled on a polo shirt and gave me a silent shrug before opening the door.

"It's none of our business."

Chapter 24

Summer was ending, the days cooling. Bored, I took a cab to Taksim. The pastry shop at the Marmara was full of families and couples. The women wore pearls and high heels.

Outside a *simit* store, a line was already forming. Girls in jeans and boys with slicked-back hair. The crowd seemed to grow by the second, now spilling onto the trolley tracks as well. I climbed down and doubled back around the mosque. A few men idled near the entrance. Another trolley was making its way up Istiklal. I waited by the stop. The trolley emptied, and new riders got on. I sat for a few minutes, thinking, then stood and began the slow walk to the fish market. Off a small alley a woman was selling tiny embroidered purses. I bent down to study them, and when I stood and turned, I walked straight into Alexandra.

She was in the abaya, but her face was uncovered.

"I've been calling your name since Taksim," she said.

"Alexandra," I said.

"How's the AC?"

"Guess."

She grimaced. "Where are you off to?"

"I need to buy a suitcase—I'm leaving Brando."

"What?" Alexandra grabbed my arm. "Just like that, without asking him about the letter?"

"I know the letter is true. I've known it for a long time. I'm just sick of this whole life."

Alexandra pushed the veil back, let her hair fall over her shoulders.

"Look, Flash, don't do anything rash," she said. "You don't know if that letter is true or—"

"I do know it's true," I said. "I found letters they'd been writing to each other. She gave him a book."

"Oh," Alexandra said. She folded her veil in her hands, unfolded it, folded it.

"Anyway, I'm leaving Istanbul," I said.

"What about Baghdad?"

"I'm through with war."

"Bullshit."

"I'm serious—even if the visa comes through, this is it, this is my last war."

"Mine just came through," Alexandra said. "It's why I was calling you. I was on my way to the American consulate. Why don't you come with me?"

"Alexandra, I appreciate it, but I don't want to think about Baghdad right now,"

"OK, fair enough," she said. She walked quickly alongside me, trying to keep up. "Did you know Isaac's back?"

"Oh?"

"Totally fucked up, I heard."

I stopped walking and turned to her. "He was injured?"

"No, mentally," she said. "He's having a welcome-back-to-purgatory party for himself this weekend."

"I'm not interested." I kept walking.

"I'll pass by and pick you up."

"No."

"Come on, Flash," she said. "Stop isolating yourself. It's not healthy."

Chapter 25

When the elevator opened at my floor, I saw that my apartment door was propped open with a toolbox. I stepped inside. I hesitated a moment, then recognized the voices; the repairmen had returned. In my bedroom, a man stood on a ladder, adjusting the screws on the air conditioner. Another man stood below, handing him tools. He looked at me when I walked in.

"Hepsi harika?" I said.

"Evet, klima."

"Does it work now?" The man stared at me for a moment and then continued to hand things up to the man atop the ladder. I flipped through my notebook, but couldn't find any useful phrase.

"Evet," I said. "Çok naziksiniz."

The men ignored me. I left them where they were. In the kitchen, I poured myself a glass of wine and carried it out to the big room. It had grown too chilly to sit outside. I was on a second glass when the repairmen walked out and spoke to me. They went on for a long time, using hand gestures and pointing up to the ceiling. When they were done, I nodded.

"Teşekkürler," I said.

"Rica ederim."

I closed the door after them and passed the lock.

They had moved the bed back to the center of the room and hung the air conditioner. I turned it on. Hot air. I let it run for a few minutes until the smell of burning plastic became unbearable. I switched it off, and took my things out to the big room. Winter was coming soon anyway. I made my bed on the couch and, still in my clothes, fell asleep at once.

Just before dawn, my cell phone woke me. I stood from the couch and began to search for it. When I finally found it atop a kitchen cabinet, the ringing had stopped. I checked the calls. Brando. I lay back on the couch, but couldn't sleep. The speakers went on in the mosque, and I braced myself for the call to prayer. When it was over, I sat where I was to watch the dawn come up, and then I made myself some coffee. When the sun was brightening the sky, the phone rang again, and I turned off the ringer.

"Tunes, man. I love you so much. Please don't leave me, you hear? Please don't. I would die without you. I mean it. I can't live without you. I love you so much. I wouldn't be able to go on without you."

The picture book lay on the coffee table where Alexandra had left it. An illustrated history of the world that someone had given us. Page 123 featured the Flavians and the

Adopted Emperors. A small insert in the bottom corner offered some words on "The Greek Philosophy of Stoicism."

I unfolded the letter and read it again. Women had been getting such letters for centuries. There was nothing original in either the impulse to write it or my reaction to it. Why then was it so devastating, why was sorrow so unbearable in the particular? Whoever wrote the letter knew nothing of the afternoon we spent on the couch as I read out passages from *Lady Chatterley's Lover*. We howled with laughter, our sides aching. Or the long bike trip through Sicily—the abandoned Greek temple, the night in Agrigento. Whoever wrote the letter didn't know the tears either, or all the times I flew to him, across continents, and he turned away from me in the dark. But Alexandra. She understood how each word could shatter the little life we built with brave face and lies. Alexandra knew.

A single sailboat glided south to the Marmara Sea. I watched it go. To be on it! Away from the memories and the arguing. To push back from the shore and not ever have to return. To float in silence. To go away from Alexandra's face, the face that had followed me all these years, to watch it grow smaller and smaller in the distance.

I unfolded my new suitcase and began to pack. My boots on the bottom, then jeans, then pants. I rolled up my shirts and tucked them into the corners. The red dress I hadn't worn in two years? I should leave that. Same with the high heels I'd bought in Bodrum and never worn. But the T-shirts, yes, the sweaters, yes. The coats also, though I wouldn't need them in Miami. I spent the next two hours folding, rolling, packing. And the ritual soothed me. Was this insight? Had I spent the last years in delusion? Could I even properly call myself a wife?

So much of my life so far had been spent waiting. Waiting for Wonderboy to come home. Waiting for the moon to rise, dinner to come, winter to give way to spring. Now, for certain now, I would go home. Contempt for him? How could he?

I packed three suitcases with clothes and shoes. My toiletries, I would leave here. I would not travel with half-empty bottles or spent perfumes. I moved the suitcases to my office. Then I fixed myself a *pastırma* sandwich. It was late for breakfast, too early for lunch. I poured myself a glass of the Turkish Gamay and took the whole thing out to the balcony. It was cool, but still bright. The water was luminous, the Asian hills gentle. Could I really leave? I finished my sandwich and sat for a while with the Gamay. It was thin and biting as usual, but even so it put me in a quiet state. To-night, I would send an e-mail to my photo agency, see if they could place me somewhere in the States, preferably Miami. Maybe the Caribbean. I'd ask my mother to check with a friend from school—did her cousin still own the wedding studio on Coral Way? I'd go back to work and be productive and happy.

I was through with wars, with travel, with Istanbul. The stupid war in Iraq. How we argued about it, as if it made any difference. How ridiculous it all seemed now. "Evil exists!"

Wonderboy had shouted. It was an important time in world history. We would rid the world of all bad, and we would be there to cover it, a team, just like always. Powell's silly chart. "A black man wouldn't lie," Wonderboy had insisted.

"Illegal war of aggression!" I shouted it so often that it became a bitter joke between us. Just like "Life is hard." And all that arguing and laughing and distance were just other ways of talking about the reasons we loved and hated each other. If we could solve the world's contradictions, our own would become clear; we could stop finally, just stop.

Chapter 26

Early Saturday morning, I went down to Cihangir and bought a few bottles of wine and some cheese for Isaac's party.

Isaac Méndez de León had moved to Istanbul a few weeks after we did. He'd called up Brando for advice, and after dinner we had ended up at his apartment for drinks. He'd made a big show of knowing my "work." A charmer, half Argentine, tall and dark, but without substance. We'd met in the chilly days of October, and I remember he was wearing white linen pants with a white linen shirt. His teeth were white against his tanned skin. He moved in a way that suggested he knew radio was a waste of his worth.

The radio guys made no money, but Isaac came from a wealthy Greenwich family. Presumably they were subsidizing his Istanbul adventure, because the Arkadaş was one of the more fashionable buildings in Gümüşsuyu. It was set into its own small plot with a beautiful garden, and its stone facade was elaborately carved.

Alexandra rang just after seven. I met her downstairs and was startled to see her out of her abaya, wearing a simple dress, her hair pulled away from her face. "Hello, Flash," she said.

Together we walked to Isaac's apartment, which was just over the hill. Isaac lived alone on the top floor, beneath the eaves. When Alexandra and I arrived at the building, the main door was open. We waited inside a few minutes for the doorman before finally calling the elevator. We took it to the seventh floor and from there walked up a narrow wooden stairway, where, following the handwritten signs, I squeezed through a series of narrow passageways that I didn't recall and motioned to Alexandra to follow.

"This sucks," she said.

I could hear her breathing heavily behind me. At the top, I crouched beneath an undersize doorway and then took a second, even more precarious stairway up. Once inside, it wasn't much better. The apartment was arranged on alternating levels, with steps leading from the bed to the hall, the bathroom to the kitchen. The whole thing was tiny and wobbly as a robin's nest.

"Oh, my God," Alexandra said. "I have to get out on the terrace. This place is like a coffin."

"Go," I said. "I'll be right there."

I waited a moment in the darkened entrance, in the shadows, watching from behind the glass. The women wore dresses and smoked. The men held their drinks close to their chests. They moved their lips soundlessly and threw open their mouths to laugh. I watched Alexandra circulate among the party, and I saw the men turn discreetly to watch her pass. In a few minutes, she was surrounded by admirers, all of them laughing and jostling to put their hands on her bare shoulders. In a corner, a group gathered around a hookah pipe, and I recognized Isaac at the center of it. I hesitated another moment. Then I stepped through the threshold and out onto the terrace.

The first thing I noticed when I slid the door aside was the noise. Laughter, shouting, everyone trying to make themselves heard above the house music. Lights had been strung across the rafters over the garden, and small white candles ran the perimeter of the terrace. Stainless steel outdoor heaters glowed here and there. I so hated journalist parties, the hilarity that barely hid its viciousness, the burned-out cases, the impossible cockiness of the new ones. Always the same questions—"Where have you been?" "What are you working on?" "Did you see so-and-so's piece, worthless . . ." It had been a mistake to come.

"Flash!" Isaac stood unsteadily and opened his arms. "Flash, *mi amor*. Thank you for coming. You are absolutely ravishing."

He stepped over the legs of his friends to make his way to me. I was embarrassed, mostly, I thought, for him.

He kissed me on both cheeks.

"Isaac, it's wonderful to see you," I said. "Actually, I came with Alexandra, who—"

"Yes!" he said. "Alexandra, who is always running for most popular." He turned to pick her out in the crowd. Then he laughed, but there was something forced, unnatural, in it.

"You look well," I said. And hated myself for always saying the same lies. Isaac was still handsome, but he looked decidedly unwell. Thin and sallow.

"I don't have the slightest idea what you're talking about, my darling," he said. "I really don't. I look like hell, *mi amor.*" He laughed again.

He took me by the hand. "Come, my beautiful dear, sit with me and be my love in the wonderful land of B——." He led me to the sofa, tripping and laughing. I didn't recognize any of the ones gathered around the hookah pipe, but Isaac demanded that they make room for me. Two young women who had been sitting on either side of him looked at each other. Did they exchange a smile?

"Really, Isaac," I said. "Don't let me interrupt."

"Nonsense! Come and partake of the splendid Turkish magic, and therefore I have sailed the seas and come to the holy city of Byzantium . . . to keep a drowsy emperor awake . . . singing masters of my soul, blah blah blah . . . Have some, Flash!"

"Thanks, I really don't smoke. I didn't plan to stay long, just was hoping to catch up and ask you about Baghdad and—"

"Hush, hush." Isaac dragged me down to the sofa next to him. His skin was hot beneath the thin linen shirt.

"The thing with the ABC translator just floored everyone," I said. "Did you know him? Who's still there?" I realized that what I was trying to get at was a question about Nadia, and as soon as I understood it, I stopped talking.

"Every crazy-ass loser in the world is still there," Isaac said. "That place is fucked up."

I'd never heard Isaac talk like that. For a journalist, he was refined, even dandy. Hearing him now was as unsettling as hearing my own mother curse.

"Do you have wine?" I said, trying to get up.

"Don't leave, lovely," he said. "Women are always leaving me."

The others laughed.

A man sitting across from me winked and shouted over the music, "Don't pay him any mind, sweetie."

Another woman took a long drag at the hookah pipe. "Isaac was telling us war stories."

The man she passed the pipe to, a short bald man that I thought I recognized, squinted at me.

"Who are you, anyway?"

"This is Flash, the great Afghan photographer," Isaac shouted. He laughed again.

"Hardly," I said.

"Are you Afghan?" the bald man asked me.

"No."

"Isaac was telling us war stories," the first woman repeated.

"Who are you with?" the bald man insisted.

"Me?"

"Flash answers to no one," Isaac said.

"Isaac was telling us war stories."

"Shut up!" Isaac's grip strengthened on me, and his face was pale in the candlelight.

The music changed tracks and started again. In the intervening silence, a dozen little conversations floated over us.

"Turn the goddamn sound down!" Isaac shouted.

The others looked at one another, but no one said anything. When the music started again, it was softer.

"For the love of God," Isaac said. "I'm half deaf now, but I can't stand all that fucking noise. You know what war is, *mi amor*? War is fucking noise, that's all it is, noise."

He had taken his hand off my arm, but he was talking to me. The hookah came my way, and I passed it. Isaac took a long drag and then drank down the rest of his glass.

"See, the thing is, Flash, I'm going to tell you the secret," Isaac said. "Here, lean closer. I don't want the others to hear, they don't understand. Outgoing and incoming, there are different ways to tell which is which by listening for the sound."

"Bombs?" I asked. Isaac's breath smelled of whiskey. I looked around for Alexandra—she was nowhere. Could she have left without me?

Isaac ignored me and continued. "It's not immediately obvious what's outgoing, so for example, your brain begins to sort out what the various sounds are, so there's artillery and there's mortars and plain shooting and bombs and machine gun fire . . . your brain starts to figure out what's what. So then you categorize: That's a bomb, because the bad guys don't have airplanes . . . and you can hear *shhooo boom*, that's outgoing so that's nothing you have to worry about . . . artillery sounds like *shoooooo boom*, clearly that's the good guys because the bad guys don't have 155 millimeter. For me, I'm always right. A car bomb, now that's totally different; a car bomb tends to be one fucking blast, big. A mortar shell is generally pretty small. With a car bomb there's nothing before, but the blast is big. From ten miles away, I can tell you a fucking car bomb, don't ask me why."

I took his hand. "Isaac—"

"Don't fucking interrupt me!" he yelled. "Sorry, *mi amor*, sorry. I'm joking. What? You don't think I'm nutso, do you?" He appealed to the others.

Shrugs. "No way! Not Isaac, man."

"Isaac's an original."

"Shut up, lackeys!" He turned to me, smiling. "This is important. The weirdest sound, I'll never forget it; it took me a week to get it. I was trying to explain it to these clowns before you got here, but no one understands. The weirdest sound was the AC-130. It's a plane, propeller-driven plane flown by . . . flown with, fuck, a cannon on it. It's an enormous cannon, which really is the end-of-the-world cannon, it's like that high. The thing comes in and you can hear the drone *mmmmmm mmmmmm*, if you're an American and it's nighttime, it's party time. It circles over the battlefield and they have infrared scope and they just look for movement that's not supposed to be there and they circle and they're taking orders, they can look and see fucking into the center of the world."

"Isaac," I said. "I need to get something to drink."

"Don't leave me, baby," he said. "Let me play my music for you."

The others laughed. One of the men stood, went into a bag, and slowly refilled the pipe. Then he laid another piece of coal in it.

"I hope you're through with Iraq," I said.

"Through, yes, absolutely," he said. "I have the best fucking bomb sound collection in the world now, so I'm through. I'm going to make that shit into an orchestra. You're going to hear what I got. I'm going to play it tonight."

One of the young women nodded her head. Her eyes were closed. "He sounds fucked up, but he's right," she said. "I've heard it."

"Damn right!" Isaac said and laughed.

"Let me just get up for a second," I said. "You have some wine? Can I bring you something?"

"Whiskey. But wait, don't leave. Wait. You should listen to my collection, Flash," he said. "Stay. I'm going to play it. I have every kind of bomb you can imagine, right here and on tape. The AC-130 is the best. Fucking chorus of angels. When it attacks, it circles in a circular position and the kick of the cannon just makes the circle wider. A tight circle, you can hear it, it sounds, I swear to God, like a souped-up version of a tennis-ball machine. *Blish, plish, plish* . . . You think, what the fuck is that thing? I thought it was a goddamn spaceship first time I heard it. There's the drone and then *pop, pop,* and then you wait and count to five, *boom, boom, boom,* and they're just wasting these fuckers . . . three seconds apart like lightning. When you figure it out, though, when we figured it out, it was kicking, man. It's us, not them, so we're cool."

I tried to stand.

"Don't leave me, baby."

"Just for a drink."

"Kiss me first."

"I'm not going to kiss you, Isaac."

"Kiss me, please." He bent over me and put his tongue in my mouth. His breath was sour, but his lips were soft, his touch gentle. I pushed him away and stood.

The others pretended to ignore us. One of the men had his hand halfway up a girl's skirt.

Isaac pulled me down, and I landed hard next to him.

"I need to find Alexandra," I said.

"Forget your friend," Isaac said, closing his eyes. "I just saw her go into the cabana with my pool guy." He laughed. Then closed his eyes. "*Mmmmm*," he said. "That's what it sounds like."

"I should go," I said.

Isaac took my hand. "You're not leaving me." He waved at a man who stood by the bar.

"Mark, bring a whiskey for me and a glass of wine for Flash here." Isaac turned to me. "You'll be fine now, just don't leave me. Red?"

I nodded.

The man by the bar handed me a glass of wine—Gamay, I could smell it—and I drank it down. I leaned back into the sofa. The night was clear.

"Isaac, did you see Brando when you were in Iraq?"

"Brando, the lone wolf," said Isaac, his voice far away and soft now.

"Was he well?"

Isaac turned to me. His speech and his movements might suggest a man barely holding himself together. But his blue eyes were calm and intelligent.

"Yeah, Flash, Brando was well," he said. "You don't need to worry."

The hookah went around again, and the next time I looked up I saw Alexandra walking toward us with Charlie, who worked for AFP, though he was American. He had his arm around her waist.

"Alex!" Isaac shouted. "Come join us. You're the next one in."

Alexandra giggled—something I had never seen her do.

"I was just in myself—for a short time," Charlie said. "Lots of bang-bang." Laughter all around.

Charlie laughed too. We made room in the circle for the two of them. Alexandra smiled strangely.

"One of the British papers just sent some twenty-four-year-old to Baghdad," Charlie said. "Kid is filing exclusively for the Web. Has some kind of blog."

A few people groaned. "Our days are numbered, dude," Isaac said. The others laughed.

"The *Post* just appointed a Web editor," one of the women said. "I don't know what the fuck he does beyond send these inane Web reports."

"We have one of those."

"The thing is, if you do the math—which no journalist is capable of, naturally—you see that the numbers don't add up. Top story gets maybe 5,000 hits, and then it's down from there. But the home page supposedly gets something like 500,000 hits." The woman paused, and the others stared blankly. "You see what I mean," she said. "If it's not stories, what are those other 495,000 people clicking on?"

"Horoscopes."

"Weather."

"Oh, man, we're really toast."

"God, I hate all that stuff," I said. "One of my agencies wanted me to get a MySpace account. What the hell is that?"

"It's one of the new media offerings to create knowledge," Charlie said in a stilted voice.

"It's like a yearbook," Alexandra said.

"Sounds stupid," I said. "Everything's become so fragmented."

"It's you who is fragmented," Alexandra said. "You live this emotionally removed life, Flash. You always have."

I was taken aback. "I don't know what you're talking about, Alexandra," I said.

"Surface living," she said. "It's like the screwing that happens in war zones. That grasping after intensity, after genuine human feeling. Because the world we've created for ourselves, the one we go longing for, just sucks."

"Whoa, whoa, whoa," Isaac said. "This is my party, and there will be no sucking. Not without my permission."

Everyone laughed, and the conversation broke up. But I was seething. With Alexandra, the bullying and the smugness were always just beneath the surface. I remembered a long-ago party in Delhi where she had humiliated a young broadcaster who had (pretentiously, it's true) quoted Goethe and mispronounced his name. Without taking leave of her elegant grace, Alexandra had responded by quoting "Go-eth's cousin *Goorta*" in German: "Er kann mich im Arsche lecken." The poor man had not an idea what she'd said while the others laughed, tears filling their eyes.

I watched her now with Charlie. He had not released her waist and held her tightly to him. I felt uncomfortable. Out of group, as my father used to say.

I'm not stupid. I know how writers feel about photographers. They think we're all dull reactionary animals. They don't see a mental process. Writers like Alexandra are especially sensitive to this question of relevance. They're all locked in the world of words and symbols. It was different for me. I saw something, and I took a picture of it. Maybe it wasn't any different: Didn't we both substitute facsimile for life? But at least I didn't have that added burden of understanding and sense to deal with. My photographs spoke for themselves. Even when I didn't always know what they were saying.

Very late, Alexandra and Charlie walked me to my apartment. I hugged her at the gate. She was disheveled, ordinary in her ordinary dress. Without the exotic pull of the abaya, she suddenly seemed just old and tired. Is that why she wore it everywhere? Without it, everyone could see that the edges of her grace were fading. I watched Charlie crush her to him, and I understood that Alexandra was as lonely as the rest of us. For the first time I saw her high-handedness as the expression of a profound and ancient isolation.

I took the stairs slowly. Upstairs, I closed the curtains. My head felt swollen with smoke and wine. It was almost morning. I collapsed in bed and then suddenly woke to what, in my still-dreaming state, I thought could be an earthquake, then became convinced was the end of the world. When I was fully awake, I realized it was just the people upstairs. The two of them were moving every piece of furniture in their bedroom, dragging them back and forth over my head. The ceiling fan swayed beneath the vibrations. I got out of bed. As soon as I stood, the moving stopped. I heard giggles. After a few minutes the moving started again; it sounded like wheels grinding, concrete tumbling, steel beams crashing into one another. Goddamn this city and its nuts. I went out into the kitchen and came back with a broom. But the ceiling was too high. I'd need a chair. I'd begun to drag one to my bedroom when I thought of the people below me. I left the chair in the middle of the hallway and went back into the room. More giggling, followed by stomping. I stripped the sheets from my bed and took them out to the couch. I lay awake, my only comfort in knowing that their retaliatory strike was also keeping them up in the middle of the night. I closed my eyes. A few hours later, the dawn call to prayer woke me from disjointed thoughts that had not quite gathered into dreams. I did not shut my eyes again, and right before sunrise, I got up, made myself some coffee, and went out to the balcony. It was cold in the darkness. I thought I heard a distant voice, *Chestnuts, warm and whole.* Then the sound of a jet followed by the quiet of a birdless early morning in Istanbul.

Chapter 27

It was our last night in Herat. I had woken in the middle of the night again and lay in the dark, listening to Brando's breathing. In the years I had known him, his night breathing had become increasingly ragged. In a few years it would progress to full-out snoring.

The moon had grown to a luminous sliver, too weak to light the room, but hopeful nevertheless in the way of new things. The next morning we would be taking the UN flight back to Peshawar with Miles and Patrice. The others planned to continue overland to Mazar-i-Sharif. I couldn't shake my anxiety, but I didn't know myself well enough to understand where it came from. That afternoon I had walked to the bazaar alone. It was the first place in Afghanistan where I had seen women gathered in public. Almost all the shoppers were women, concealed beneath their flowing bright burkas, grimy at the hems. I'd brought just a small pocket camera that I could hide in the folds of my *kameez*. But it was impossible to do any shooting. In my veil and sunglasses, I was instantly recognized as a Western woman, and since most of the westerners in Herat then were aid workers, I soon was surrounded by identical burkas, disembodied voices speaking to me first in French, then in English. They wanted jobs, help, someone to listen to how they went from being university professors to ghosts overnight. A woman grabbed my wrist. I could barely make out her eyes, moist and dark, behind the fabric mesh of her burka. "Please, sister, tell me, do you think Iran will invade?" Liberation from Iran—she was hopeful. It was hot and dusty, and the pleadings of the women should have moved me, but instead they repulsed me, reminding me of all that was weak and hopeless in our sex, how easy it was to be trampled into oblivion, how when things fell apart it was brute strength that mattered.

I lay in bed listening to Wonderboy. Had I chosen our life, or had he? Or had neither of us chosen at all? Afghanistan, that land of myth and superstition, upended my notions, laid bare all the myth and superstition I had been raised to take as fact. In the remote places of Afghanistan, the certainty of fate was truth, and the idea that one could remake oneself and be rewarded for it in this world was a fantasy cooked up by savages.

Candlelight from the hallways flickered beneath the door. The house was silent, not even a floorboard creaked, all the others in bed and dreaming. What was the time? Two? Three in the morning? The flight to Peshawar was early, and I still hadn't packed. I would be exhausted. I was always exhausted now, the endless packing, flying, disembarking, unpacking, washing, packing, flying. My life was running out. I was asleep half the time, and bone weary the other. I stood and made my way to the bathroom on tiptoe.

The candle by the tub sputtered. I squatted over the toilet, and when I was done I wiped down the seat. Then, out of habit, I turned the spigot on the faucet, forgetting that the guesthouse had been dry for the last two days. But to my delight, a trickle of water fell. I couldn't remember the last time I had been so pleased—all of us had collected layers of grime and sweat that we tried to dilute with precious bottled water. Now, grateful, I stripped off my nightshirt and splashed handfuls of water on my neck, my shoulders. It smelled of metal, but the water was cold, and my clean new shivering seemed a happy promise. The hot anxiety peeled off drop by drop. I splashed quickly, afraid it wouldn't last. I was rubbing my eyes with a corner of my nightshirt when I heard the bathroom door creak open. I gave a small jump back and caught myself.

"American lady."

Chapter 28

Did he tell Alexandra? Brando and I had left for Peshawar a few hours later without saying good-bye to the others. It was still dark when we boarded our flight. Wonderboy held my hand in the back of the plane, knowing how I hated the single-engine props. The UN pilots, war-tired cowboys who seemed to be chasing their last great adventure in death, ignored a small-craft shutdown at the Peshawar airport. The plane tumbled and rose in the windstorm, once falling so hard and fast through the air that g-forces stuck our heads to the seats. So this is how it ends, I thought, so much time wasted. We landed, and that night I couldn't sleep, thinking about the brief banality of our days: the human being, dumb creature that he is, is convinced of his overwhelming intelligence, first among beasts. And for what? To build cities and machines, to dream and conquer and destroy so that we can end no better than the cats of the savannah, who at least have the good sense to spend their time on earth resting, eating, and screwing. I forgot this almost immediately, though. You can't live all your life in your head. You can't out-smart your programming, so why try? Within hours, I was sucked back into all the human striving and planning, the desire to pay lip service to the good while making obsessive notes of the world's decay.

Months later I heard Amir had disappeared near Bamiyan. The circumstances were unclear. Someone said he had ridden into battle with a death wish like some kind of Afghan José Martí. From someone else, I heard he had joined the Northern Alliance, had become a confidant of Massoud's. Later, when I heard he had shot himself in the stomach—by accident, supposedly—I remembered the gun he had produced for the camel. His words: *It is a good sound*. I had no right to mourning, so why did my throat tighten to remember how he had turned suddenly to me by the sputtering light of the candle?

Had he told her before he vanished? Did Alexandra know? The suspicion returned, that letter. *What do you get out of that life anyway?*

More than a week passed without word from Alexandra. I found myself going for longer and longer walks, and gradually realized that I was looking for her. Had she noticed my irritation at Isaac's? It now seemed so silly. I was tired and annoyed at other things. I should try to get in touch with her. I was surprised to admit it: I missed her. I was about to call

Isaac to find out if he'd heard from her when I got an e-mail from Alexandra:

> Flash, dearest, had to scramble to get this flight to
> Amman and didn't have time to say bye–bye. Will
> write from Hell. xxooo

Dearest. I didn't believe her. I shuffled the memories now like photographs, one over the other: the Bebek, the trolley, the coffeehouse, the tower. That night I had chased her near Istiklal? Was she heading home? Or following me? I returned to the Bebek, sat out on the deck day after day hoping that life could work like a tape and I could rewind it to the spot where Alexandra crosses the darkened lobby, her strides long and ungainly. Except this time I rise and follow her, through the empty streets, past the ware-less merchants, back into the broken past we shared, right back to that guesthouse in Herat.

Chapter 29

In September, the sweetest figs start coming into season, my favorite time in Istanbul. The trees on my street were heavy with them, the ground below sticky with fallen fruit. I was at the market, sorting through the first offerings, when my phone rang. Brando, calling from the roof. He would not be coming home this month after all. "I understand," I said. "It's an important time in world history." He didn't hear the irony in my voice. Before we hung up, he said, "Don't forget I love you, Tunes." He hadn't asked me to join him. Had he given up? Or was he occupied?

"Tunes," he said. "Can I ask you something?"

"Sure."

"Is everything all right?"

"Why wouldn't it be?"

"I don't know," he said. "You seem— Nothing. I'm just tired. Don't pay any attention to me."

"What's the matter?"

"Nothing," he said. "I love you."

I put the phone in my pocket, paid for the figs, and began to walk. But instead of going home, I headed down to Tünel. Outside the coffeehouse, I sat on a bench to eat my figs. When I was done, I sat for a long time. The afternoons were growing cool. Soon it would be winter. I watched the young people come and go in the plaza. I studied their faces. Every last one of them strangers. How big the world was, and how alone each of us was in it.

I crumpled the paper bag and stood to throw it away, and that's when I saw her cross the trolley tracks and go into the funicular station.

I almost called out, but instead I stood where I was, paralyzed by the usual indecision. Then, scarcely thinking, I ran after her. I got to the platform just as the train was pulling away. It was no use waiting for the next one. I ran back out, down the steps, and hailed a cab at the light district. I pointed across the Golden Horn. Çabuk, I said. We sped through the streets and into the tunnel. On the other side, I handed him a wad of bills and shouted, "Çok naziksiniz!" I ran all the way to the funicular station and descended the steps two at a time. I reached the bottom panting. The platform was empty except for three teenagers with punk haircuts. They stopped talking and looked up at me. The train had come and gone. Back up to the street, where the setting sun dazzled the mosque. Rush hour, hundreds of people on foot. I would never find her. I began to walk to the bridge. The men were lined up along the railings, fishing. I usually avoided the bridge—terrified of being hooked. Beyond them, men squatted before blankets, selling leather cell-phone holders, phone cards, key chains. The whole city was a giant hustle. I lifted my eyes. The traffic was backed up on the little bridge, the city caught in a late-sun haze. And then, up ahead, bobbing through the crush of people, moving quickly, the woman in the black abaya.

I followed, mumbling, "Pardon, pardon." When she came to the end of the bridge, she turned right. She had not turned back once, but I was afraid of getting too close. I wanted her to lead me home. I followed through the streets. This must have been the plumbing district Erkan had driven me through months before; table after table was covered with pipes in different shapes and materials. At the end of the street she turned left, past the marina. She was walking quickly, and I didn't want to lose her. Fortunately, she stood out in the abaya, and several times people turned to watch her go. I would say Amir's name and wait for her reaction. I would catch her. Then I would ask her about the letter.

The street ended at a collection of *nargile* cafés. The woman lifted the hem of her abaya and climbed the sidewalk. A man sitting at an outdoor table waved her over. Before she joined him, I shouted, "Alexandra." She didn't turn around, and I ran to close the distance. "Alexandra!"

She kept walking. But now the man had noticed me and stood, pointing. She didn't turn around. When she got to the man, he bent down and whispered something. I was two feet away. She finally turned, her chin thrust out. She was the right size and shape. Her face was covered—only her dark eyes were visible.

"Alexandra?"

I got very close. She responded in Turkish.

"I know it's you," I said. But I was less certain.

The man held his hand out to stop me from coming closer and said something stern and guttural.

"I'm sorry," I said. I took a step back. "I thought—Alexandra, if it's you, I need to talk to you. It's very important."

The woman shook her head. Her eyes narrowed. Incomprehension.

"Sorry to have bothered you," I said, addressing the man. "Pardon."

I bowed and then straightened, watching them. The man put his hand on the woman's back to lead her away.

Back on the street, I stood very close to the road, feeling the terrible rush of air with each car. The noise was unbearable: car horns, deep rumbling buses, the *whoosh whoosh* of machines driven by people desperate to return home, to pour themselves a drink, to forget. Everywhere the smell of diesel fuel and smoke, and behind it, like a distant memory of childhood, a faint scent of the sea, of what this city had once been and would be again when man finished burning out his last days.

There was a full moon that night, and I sat on the couch with a bottle of white wine to wait for it to come up. The Bosporus was dark. On the far shore, the electric lights moved and shifted. At first the moon was only a bright fingernail behind the hills. And then the rest rose, heavy and round, unassailable.

Chapter 30

The flickering light moved over him like gold dust. His pupils were round and black. I could hear my breathing in the small bathroom, the click of the door shutting.

When I was a teenager, my mother had told me, "Don't let them get close. Even if you're both standing, he can slip inside you." It was meant as a warning, but the image thrilled me, and for weeks I could think of little else.

I backed against the console. He reached forward. Stopped. I stood still, but nodded in the dark. He started again. *American lady.* He rolled down my pajama bottoms slowly, murmuring something I couldn't understand. "Amir," I whispered. He kissed my feet, my knees. He straightened, resting his hands on either side of me now. I slid my palms down his forearms slowly, stopping, starting again, stopping. His arms were covered with ridges, scars. He wrapped his arms around me, lifted me. I held him. The candlelight cast a trembling shadow over the door. He pressed deeper into me, kissed me below my ear. "They are from love," he whispered.

When I returned to bed, electric and alive, I was glad, for the first time, of the way Brando instinctively moved away from me in his sleep.

I am a photographer. I make pictures from the moments people forget, the moments that are gone in an instant. In an opening and shutting of the lens. I take that one moment and force you to look, to see in a way you wouldn't on your own. And you come back for more. All we create aspires to the condition of love, that state when the senses are heightened, when everything—even the rotting and sorrowful—is pregnant with meaning and light. I have tried to explain what war is, what it does. I've been telling myself this is the story, my theme: the great tragedy of existence, of annihilation and destruction. But all this time what I've been recording is the end of desire. The terrible violence at the end of love.

Chapter 31

The story is well known by now. Wonderboy was killed on his first trip home from Baghdad. October 9, 2003, a Thursday. It was supposed to be a surprise—his return. I hadn't even done the groceries.

I was on Istiklal, still searching for Alexandra, when Alif called me. "Are you at home?" Her voice was strange, deep. For the first time I noticed her accent.

She asked me to meet her in twenty minutes at the coffeehouse next to Rafik's.

"What's going on?"

She hesitated. "I need to tell you something."

I still didn't get it. I thought Alif wanted to tell me about Nadia, and all the old anger stirred in me again, the stupid betrayal.

"Alif, I really don't want—"

"Please. It's important."

She hung up before I could respond.

❁ ❁ ❁

Alif was sitting near the back, and it took me a while to recognize her. There was a man with her. When I waved, neither one waved back. They looked at each other, and the man stood. That's when I knew.

He was a doctor at the American hospital. I learned later that everyone was afraid I would hurt myself. Throw myself from the balcony. They didn't know me. But I didn't know myself either.

An improvised explosive device. A roadside bomb. The airport road was dangerous. One of the bodyguards also dead. My ears buzzed. Not Wonderboy. Wonderboy was never going to die. Never. He wasn't a kid. He knew war. If I had been there. If I had told him to come home right after I got that letter. If I had insisted. Come home, Brando. This has gone far enough. Not dead. A mistake, someone else's husband. Someone else's life. Not me sitting here, not you and your goddamn shrink. Check the facts again. Don't come to me with this bullshit. He called a week ago, said he couldn't come home. Idiots! I would have made him dinner, I would have had dinner waiting for him and a glass of gin and tonic. That's what he likes. That's what he always drinks on the first night back from an assignment. Ask him, ask Wonderboy about it. He'll tell you. Isn't that right, Tunes?

❊   ❊   ❊

We buried him in Miami. The papers said how strong I was. They didn't realize that it was all a mistake. Brando wasn't dead.

My mother wanted me to stay—someone would pack up the Istanbul apartment for me. Stay here and rest. But days later I returned to the city. It made no sense, so I didn't tell anyone: I thought Wonderboy would be waiting for me, all alone in that glass-walled apartment, worried about where I'd gone.

Chapter 32

I returned to Istanbul in late October. But the scent of sweet fruit lingered in the crowded streets and alleyways all the way to the water's edge. Here and there men sold bananas and pears by the road. Months before, the same men had sold green plums and cherries from the same wooden carts. Soon would come the chestnuts, roasted over red coals.

My first morning back, I started walking and didn't stop until I was at the bottom of Istiklal. It was cold. I had a coffee at Kahvehaus, and then I took the trolley back up to Taksim. I knew the trip so well now: Paşabahçe, where I had bought all that glassware. The school for rich boys, the church of San Antuan, the Benetton, the coffeehouse where teenagers spilled out of the double-wide doors, speaking English. The *simit* store with its line of schoolchildren. The trolley rattled on its tracks and slowed in front of the old mosque. A few people got off. More people crowded in. I was leaving all this behind, and almost everything else too: the Wedgwood china that we'd gotten for our wedding, the leather couch, the oak dining table. As the trolley started again, three boys ran up behind it, giggling. I watched, holding my breath as the first one leaped and caught on to the back of the car just as it gathered speed. The boy clung to the railing as he called out to the others. His voice was high and light, like song.

I spent that first week back in a numb haze. I hardly had the energy to pour the wine now. The packing boxes lay everywhere, empty. My mother was flying out in a few days. I didn't want to see her. I didn't want to see anyone. But I lacked the energy to protest.

Then, Saturday morning. A sound, a distant pop. The concussion rattled the glass in my bedroom. Less than a minute later, the sirens.

I understood right away. It was like getting a shot of something, some electric drug. Everything became clear and clean: big bomb, big story, move. I grabbed two camera bodies and checked the light. Blue skies. The bedroom clock read 9:37. I gathered my things quickly: the card wallet, two zooms. Where were the extra batteries? I should have emptied the cards. My ID. Notebook. Pens. The 285—just in case.

I ran the whole way, following the smoke.

The police were already setting up barricades. Beyoğlu— I knew the neighborhood of foreigners, named after the old gentleman's son. Months ago, Alexandra had taken me down the cobblestoned alleys in search of the tower. We had passed the synagogue, discreet and peaceful on that blazing street of light.

I slipped around the hotel, down a steep narrow alley, turned. Down another street. Sirens, women sobbing. Across to where the smoke was thick. The air smelled of cleaning solution, sharp and chemical. Chunks of concrete lay everywhere, and water spurted from broken pipes. I ran past bodies covered in white ash. Glass underfoot, shards that caught the light. A man selling shoes. A sign of a plastic Turk, holding up a menu. And then I started to shoot. I shot wildly, by instinct, not seeing the image. Feeling it. Hunting it.

Two men suspended in time as they carry a third on a salvaged door.

A bloody hand.

An old woman, head covered in a flowered scarf, mouth open in a scream.

A sliver of blue sky above the tangled gray.

Water spilling from burst pipes onto a mangled corpse.

Two women, eyes closed, hands over their mouths.

A man with his clothes burned off, hand stretched to heaven.

A child wearing a blue shirt at a window reflecting fire.

Two men covered in blood, running to the camera.

A crowd of men, some shirtless and bloodied, others strangely calm.

A woman regarding her hand, one finger missing.

A woman bent over a figure without legs.

A policeman weeping.

War without end.

I shoot past every decency, beyond care; I shoot though I can hear the policeman shouting at me above the sirens. I shoot with the tears running down my face. Oh, Brando, Brando, my Wonderboy, my sweet boy wonder.

Epilogue

In the autumn of 2007, India moved police and troops to the border with Nepal. It had already been a busy year, with conflicts in Darfur and the Sudan, broken peace plans in Sri Lanka, a resurgent Taliban in Afghanistan. And of course, the lost campaign in Iraq, where men and money vanished chasing after a president's folly.

I was on my way to Delhi, the first time I'd be back in nearly a decade. From there I'd travel to Kathmandu, pick up some color for a glossy, and then fly on to Hong Kong for a brief vacation before heading to Thailand for another assignment.

I was tired. But I was looking forward to a seven-hour layover in Schiphol, one of the world's great airports. Anyone who says all airports are the same has not really traveled. All the world's airports are not the same: the last time I flew out of Kabul, the runway was lined with bombed-out aircraft, and the Taliban had tried to stick me in a supply closet— their improvised "family" waiting room.

Schiphol was not Kabul. Schiphol was everything the chaotic outside world wasn't; it was the calm, well-designed hub at the center of madness. Travel had gone to hell since 9/11. On the day I left, JFK had been a mess. Some new threat, maybe, or the usual old ones. Lines to check in, lines for the screening. Homely barefoot people everywhere. Layers upon layers of checks. It was the same all over the world now, but knowing that never made the particular indignities of flying any easier to bear.

We landed in Amsterdam just after nine in the morning, local time, three hours behind schedule because of the delays in New York. The pilot waited on the runway for a gate, and then we slid into the cool glass comfort of the airport.

The Dutch know how to do things, and Schiphol is the soaring monument to their orderly vision of humanity. You come off the cramped plane into an airy, welcoming space. The ceilings are high, the windows clean. It's an illusion, but in a travel-induced fog it's easy to believe that someone finally figured out how to sort the ideal world from the one laced with cold and bitter disorder.

I had checked all my equipment and was traveling with just a light bag in anticipation of a good stroll through the stores. Like many airports in the West now, Schiphol is a miniaturized city, and walking through it, I thought of the man who had managed to live in an airport for years, an extended layover that wanted for nothing except, perhaps, a comfortable bed and the love of family. Every airport should have a small brass bust to him, a kind of religious shrine for the modern penitent.

I stopped at a café for an espresso and a berry pastry. A couple seated next to me whispered to one another in French, small pleasantries about the trip that was now ending for them. Across the way, a sprawling family arranged themselves around two tables. The woman who must have been the mother wore a purple hat, and she was sleek and lovely above the tumult. One of the children, a boy, sat on the marble floor, pushing two toy trucks into each other.

"Stop that," the mother said in a cultivated British accent. "You're crashing the cars."

"Mother," the boy replied, a little exasperated, "I'm *trying* to crash the cars."

The duty-free stores sold wines and meat and face creams and bonbons for families on the other side. I had five hours until my flight, and that was assuming no delays. I pushed my handcart from one store to the next. Cashmere sweaters, perfumes, chocolates, wines—the usual exports of Airport Land. At one store, I bought three boxes of chocolates from Belgium. Gifts, though I had no one in particular in mind. I waited to have them wrapped. I would be in Delhi for a few days. Perhaps I should call in on some old friends. As I stood, making plans for my arrival and otherwise daydreaming, a family passed me. The man was weighed down with bags, and the woman pushed a baby in a stroller. He wore jeans and a white shirt. She was dressed in a long skirt and a sleeveless blouse, her long black hair worn loose over her bare shoulders. I watched them go. They stopped in front of the duty-free entrance, and then the woman broke away, guiding the stroller up to a display of face creams. Already I had recognized the walk, though I had yet to register it consciously. But when she turned so that her face was in profile, I finally recognized Alexandra. She stood in front of the display, one hand on the stroller, rocking it.

The face was fuller. But it was definitely Alexandra's. I took my chocolates and thanked the clerk in English. I pushed my cart out of the store and into the hallway. I passed her slowly and then doubled back.

"Alexandra."

Her hand on the stroller stopped moving, but she didn't turn around.

I rolled my cart next to her.

"Alexandra Truso."

She pivoted, turning her face first and then her body. She maneuvered the stroller in front of her. The baby looked up at me. A little boy, dressed in blue.

We stood facing each other. For a moment I thought she would answer in a foreign language, say that I was mistaken, that she had no idea who I was. But then she smiled.

"Flash," she said. "I can't believe it."

The father joined us. He had an open, friendly face. And he didn't wait for Alexandra to introduce us.

"Francisco Cova," he said, extending his hand and giving me a warm, firm shake.

"Darling, this is Flash—I've told you about her." Alexandra paused to give him a searching look. "We've been friends forever."

"Pleasure," I said. "Truly is. And you, my dear," I said, turning to Alexandra, "you're radiant."

"That would be because of me," Francisco said and laughed.

He spoke with an accent. Was it possible? I looked at Alexandra. "It's amazing that we should run into you," she said. "Francisco and I are on our way home from Istanbul. We were there for the biennial. Frank is an artist—actually works with photos."

Francisco laughed. "You could say that," he said. "Photomontage. But next year it will be something else."

He was very tall, and his hair was cut close to his head. He wore a goatee that set off a perfect set of white, straight teeth.

"I can't believe it's you, Flash," Alexandra said. "I've been thinking of you."

"It's been a while," I said.

We stood for a moment in silence.

"Well," Francisco said, spreading his arms. "Why don't Marco and I go look for some ice cream and leave you two girls to catch up?"

Alexandra seemed to hesitate.

"Oh, please don't let me interrupt you," I said. "I don't want you to miss your flight."

"Not at all," Francisco said, and he was already taking the stroller from Alexandra. "We don't leave until tonight. You know the airport cabal wants you to spend as much idle time as possible shopping for worthless crap. Nothing like a captive audience of travel zombies."

Alexandra laughed, then kissed Francisco. "You're a dear," she said.

Alexandra linked her arm in mine and said, "Well, well, dearest Flash, alone again, just like old times. Who would have thought—here in Schiphol."

We walked down one of the spotless shining corridors. Alexandra looked relaxed and lovely, happier than when I had last seen her. A big yellow diamond rested sideways on her finger.

She'd met her husband in Madrid, on one of her leaves from Baghdad. At the time, he was doing a residency at one of the colleges. Alexandra stopped to open her wallet. She held out a photo of the two of them in Barcelona, La Sagrada Familia in the background. "This was right after we met," she said. "It was so crazy, traveling with him on an overnight train to Barcelona," she said. "But it seemed perfectly logical at the time."

Francisco with his arm around Alexandra. He was jovial and handsome even in a snapshot, silver hair beginning at the temple. Alexandra closed her wallet and smiled at me.

"It's good to see you, Flash," she said. "It really is."

"It's good to see you," I said. I watched her as she spoke. Alexandra was no longer the great beauty I had known in Delhi. But in the years since we'd last met, something had been added. She had acquired the deep voice and the quiet, restful hands of a well-loved woman.

It was not yet noon, but we managed to find a café serving beer and wine. Alexandra ordered sparkling water, and I took a glass of Malbec.

"Well," she said, and hesitated. "You look great."

I laughed. "I know I'm all beat up," I said. "It's OK. You don't have to lie."

"I tried to call you," she said. "After Brando—"

"It's OK."

She had read about it, she said, Brando's death and then the whole business of the letter when the details came out in my suit against the paper. I didn't want to talk about it. That story was over for me.

"You still believe I wrote the letter," she said.

"It doesn't matter anymore."

"It does to me," she said.

"Forget about it," I said.

"I want you to know it wasn't me."

"Look, Alexandra. I know you didn't write the letter," I said. And then continued. "It was a colleague of his."

Alexandra nodded. "Sue Chasso—I read about it. But was it really her?" Alexandra leaned forward so slightly. She still couldn't resist a good story.

"It was her, all right."

"It's just that I saw this thing where she was quoted," Alexandra said. "Her denial was pretty convincing, I have to say that—"

I cut her off. "It was her, no doubt at all."

"Oh?" Alexandra said. "She made out like the victim, and I just thought—"

"She had written a draft on her laptop," I said quickly. "Then she paid some kind of service to erase it. Made out like the computer had gotten a virus."

"Oh?"

"They must have already suspected her. Because when she went back to New York, the tech people took a look."

"But the hard drive had been erased," Alexandra said. "I don't understand."

I smiled. "Yeah, that's what she thought. And that's what she'd paid for. But you know what? Stuff is never really erased. That's what people don't realize. You think it's gone forever, but it stays in the memory. If you have a good tech guy, nothing is ever truly lost."

Alexandra looked at me strangely.

"Look, I don't know the first thing about computers," I said. "This is just what they told me. Don't ever put anything on your hard drive that might come back to haunt you."

"Flash," Alexandra said. And stopped.

"What?"

"Nothing."

The café had begun to fill with hungry travelers. It might be the middle of the night where they came from, but at

Schiphol the clock said noon, and that meant lunch. The waitress came by, asking in flawless English if we wanted anything else. Alexandra ordered another water, and I ordered another glass of Malbec.

"The letter wasn't true, you know," she said after a moment.

"You can't know that," I said.

"I just know it wasn't."

"I don't want to talk about that anymore," I said.

"OK," Alexandra said. But she remained quiet.

When I could no longer bear the silence, I said, "You look rested and relaxed. Especially for the mother of a toddler."

"Well," she said, "Francisco is wonderful. Nothing makes sense, but I'm OK. Imagine me—a new mother at forty-two. And married to another Spaniard, of all things."

"I saw a short story of yours in the *Review* a few months back," I said.

"I'm writing again," she said. She watched me, started to say something, and then stopped. "How are you doing now, really?" she said. "You OK?"

"Pretty much."

"I can't imagine," she began. "I mean, you two seemed—"

"It's OK," I said. "I really don't want to talk about it."

"I'm sorry," she said.

I was quiet. The wine had softened me. Schiphol was such a warm womb. I was so grateful to everyone who made it so.

"Don't be."

"I should have called."

I was going to tell her again to forget it. But after a moment, I gave in, sinking back into the chair.

"You know, I dreamed about it before it happened," I said.

Alexandra shook her head.

"It's true. It was December 2001." I spoke slowly, caught in the dream of my recollection. "I'd left Wonderboy in Afghanistan to attend my cousin's wedding in Miami. I was sleeping in my old room—diplomas and grade-school awards covered the walls. I closed my eyes and opened them. The ceiling curved, weighted with time. The phone rang. There was a lot of noise on the line, and then a voice said, 'He's dead. Brando's dead.'

"I collapsed, suffocating. No, no, no, no, no, no, no. I didn't know the mind could manufacture such a perfect simulacrum of grief," I said.

We sat in silence. We talked. Alexandra sighed. She told me about their neighborhood, their friends. Francisco was gone for a few days every month. He called and wrote every day, sent flowers.

"It sounds ideal," I said.

"It's not," Alexandra said. "But it's life."

I waited before responding. "I don't think Brando ever loved me," I said finally. "I left a career for him. But he was only interested in wars. His favorite thing was to go away."

Alexandra looked up. "Is that what you think?"

I shrugged. "I don't know."

We ordered lunch, two chicken sandwiches.

"Have you been back to Istanbul since the bombings?" she asked.

"No."

"This was my first time back," she said. "I wouldn't have gone if it hadn't been for Frank's show."

"Why not?"

"I don't know," she said. "Istanbul had all the wrong associations . . ." She trailed off. "But the biennial was worth it. They've opened a new modern art museum, you know, near the Galata bridge."

"Oh?"

"It's an interesting space. You would like it. It's worth catching the show if you have time. There's this arresting installation—*The House of Realization*. Ken Lum, do you know his work?"

I shook my head.

"He had this Yunus Emre poem reflected in glass, which in turn reflected the viewer, which in turn was secretly observed by a whole other group of people through a two-way mirror."

She opened her purse and took out a notebook and began reciting. " 'We encountered the house of realization, we witnessed the body. The whirling skies, the many-layered earth, the seventy-thousand veils, we found in the body. The night and the day, the planets, the words inscribed in the holy tablets, the hill that Moses climbed, the temple, and Israfil's trumpet we observed in the body. Torah, Psalms, gospel, Quran—what these books have to say we found in the body.

Everybody says these words of Yunus are true. Truth is wherever you want it. We found it all within the body.'"

Alexandra closed her notebook and looked up at me.

"All those years of my claustrophobia . . . ," she said. "I was looking at everything backward."

I smiled. "I'm glad you're writing again," I said. "Because you never did know how to have a conversation without telling a story."

The waitress set our sandwiches down. Alexandra smiled and put her notebook away.

"Where are you off to now?" she said.

"Delhi, then Kathmandu."

"The Maoists."

I nodded, chewing.

"You're still traveling," she said.

I shrugged. "For a whole year after, I didn't even get on a plane. I moved to Miami and took a job at the paper. It was like sleepwalking. Shots of dogs in baby strollers, angry homeowners, visiting officials. That's what passes for photojournalism today."

"It doesn't sound so bad," Alexandra said. "It's part of life."

"Not mine," I said.

"Is that so," she said.

"I was bored to tears," I said. "I didn't want to live like that."

She put down her sandwich and watched me. She seemed to consider something, and then she pushed back from the table.

"That's how he used to talk also," she said. "Amir."

I took a sip of wine.

"You remember him?" she said. She smiled a little and watched me.

"Of course," I said.

"You're frowning," she said. "Don't worry—he's not dead. I don't know where that story started. Just because a man carries a gun doesn't mean he's always going to use it. That's only in Chekhov."

She smiled again, a hint of that old smugness I never liked.

"He's some kind of minister now," she said. "A superstar in Karzai's inner circle, I hear. Which doesn't surprise me— he was always a supreme calculator."

I didn't say anything.

"He used to say, 'Death on a full belly is better than a life of hunger.'"

She paused, watching me, always Alexandra watching me.

There was a pleasant din to the café now, punctured occasionally by a smooth inoffensive voice announcing flights in four languages.

She watched me for a long time. I looked away. I was beginning to feel ill. "You know, Flash," she said after a time. "He told me all about it."

I looked back at her. Her gaze was steady.

"Of course," I said evenly.

"I actually felt sorry for you," she said. She leaned forward, voice lowered. "I did, Flash. I felt sorry for you. You've been around Americans too long. You don't understand the rest of the world. You don't know how people relate, the layers of intercourse, the many ways to inflict pain. Americans are so bluntly straightforward. That's why they've been so screwed over in Iraq. All those fixers and translators and native consultants are taking them for the ride of their lives. And they don't even know it. The way you didn't know it, Flash. The way you never understood the difference between love and cruelty."

I stood.

"Well, I've had quite enough," I said. I gathered my things.

"I knew he wanted to humiliate you," Alexandra continued. "But I was also fucking pissed. I'm not going to lie. I'm not afraid of admitting that. You had a husband. You had a sweet life. But you were always putting yourself off as some kind of martyr, like your thing was all about sacrifice."

I was shaking. I didn't want to hear what Alexandra had to say, but I could not move from where I stood.

"That night that I waited for you at your apartment—you were still full of that self-righteousness," she said. "What was it you said about Nadia? Something about moralizers having no problem breaking the rules when they know they aren't going to be caught."

She looked at me, unblinking. "I thought that was really rich." Then she smiled and considered me, started to say something, and stopped. After a moment she said, "You know, Flash, I didn't go to Istanbul to see you, but when I learned you were there, all that old anger came back. I wanted to confront you. I wanted you to hurt. And then I found you in a trance after that letter—caught between glimmers of your own hypocrisy and that sorrow that I also knew."

"Why, Alexandra? Why are you doing this now?"

"Because the only reason you believed that stupid letter was because it described your own betrayal."

"Alexandra, look . . . ," I said and couldn't finish.

Alexandra held her hand up. "Please."

"I never planned—"

"Don't," she said. "Don't make it worse."

I sat down, trying to overcome a sudden dizziness. Had I always been such a coward?

I had some wine left and finished it in one gulp. I needed another glass. I busied myself trying to find the waitress. I would have another quick wine and then go. I flagged the busboy and pointed to my glass. When I looked back at Alexandra, she was watching me.

"I told you I met Brando in Kabul after the invasion," she said. "You had already flown back to Miami."

I nodded and swallowed. My legs were heavy. I didn't want to hear the rest, and I could not put off hearing it any longer.

Alexandra brought her hands together and looked at them as she clasped and unclasped them.

"Everyone was staying at the old Intercon, and every night we'd all gather for drinks. You remember that cavernous old dining room on the—"

"Did you sleep with him?"

Alexandra continued calmly, ignoring me: "The old dining room on the far side of the hotel, after you crossed the lobby. It hadn't changed in thirty years. When I lived there in the nineties, it was a sad empty space; now suddenly it was packed every night—aid workers, diplomats, spooks, us. The staff had hidden all the booze in the basement when the Taliban came through, and now they were pulling stuff up. Years old. Incredible stuff, old French wines, cognacs, Russian vodka."

I stared at her.

She met my gaze, unashamed. She spoke slowly, as if English were her second language. "One night, after I don't know how many vodka tonics, I followed Brando to his room. My thinking wasn't right. It was war, no? Everyone jumping into everyone's bed. That's how it is, isn't it? If you're going to die, you might as well live. Death on a full belly . . ."

She looked away briefly and then straight at me. "And, yes, a chance to become you, to accommodate your longing, make it mine."

"A chance to fuck my husband. Say what you mean for once."

"He was already in his boxers when I got to the door. He opened it without embarrassment. I was inside the room before I noticed his confusion."

I closed my eyes.

"He turned me down," Alexandra said softly. "Brando turned me down. I offered him one night without regrets or promises, and he mumbled some excuse and went to bed alone."

I turned away and wiped my face. I didn't care about anything anymore, nothing mattered to me, the whole lot of them could go to hell. But Alexandra would not see me cry.

"He was loyal to you, Flash."

A good photograph already contains all the elements you need to understand it; all that's missing is the viewer who will project his loneliness and failure or joy or wisdom onto the flat surface of that make-believe world. I used to think life was like that—a long-developing dream. But every day, mystery eats away at the composition, blank spaces appear, whiteouts. I knew that I could not escape. I knew that I would never understand everything. But I also knew that wherever in the world I lived, Alexandra would return to make me remember.

I turned and started walking. I still hear her calling after me: "You're too in love with your own victimhood, Flash. You don't understand that Brando gave you the war you always wanted."

I didn't respond, just kept walking. I was too exhausted to cry now, too exhausted for vengeance or regret, too worn out to do anything else with my life but just keep moving, and Alexandra knew it.

He never left me. I still wake some mornings and feel his breathing next to me. Our life together plays out in moments that leave me spent and longing. Good and bad—that's how

I sorted it all out in the beginning. Now those remembrances are nothing so neat, though vastly simpler: they were just us, the entirety of us in the imperfect ever-shifting fullness that separates the living from the dead.

He had missed my cousin's wedding to finish covering the Afghan invasion. He was too deep into it by then. He landed in Miami a few days before Christmas. I picked him up in the airport and knew instantly that something had changed, that a part of him had gone away forever.

On Christmas Eve, my family cooked outside. We all sat in the backyard—my mother and father both came together for the occasion, as they did every year, more happy than when they were married. Wonderboy drank the gin and tonic I'd prepared for him. He was charming and funny. Everyone loved him. But he could not bring himself to hold my hand.

Near midnight, two short explosions next door drowned out the music. Brando leaped from his seat and tried to pull me to the ground.

"It's just fireworks," I said. "They do it every year."

"Oh, God," he said. "I'm sorry." He was pale, and when he stood, I saw that his left knee gave him trouble.

I didn't move to help him. A failure that haunts me still.

I don't remember much of that first year after his death. I wasn't really living either; some days I thought I had changed places with him, wandered into an underworld of vague plans, fears, tempests. I found no joy in work. I could barely drag myself in. The idiotic assignments oppressed me. It's what happens when you try to run away from grief—it finds you in every mundane detail of every mundane day. It was a long, slow return, and though I can't pinpoint the hour, I remember that it started when I finally gave myself over to how things were, stopped fighting or pretending.

I was working the Saturday-night shift when the guy monitoring the police radio reported a major collision on northbound I-95 at the MacArthur. It was less than a mile from the paper, and I got there before the cops. Three cars and a motorcycle. I shot for more than an hour, close-ups: the flash bleaching all nuance, bringing the broken details out of shadow. I recorded the essence: blood, bone, steel. The paper didn't print any of it. I had not expected them to, and I knew I would be mentioned in the meeting the next day. Less than a month later, I quit. Burnout—that's what everyone said. But I knew the truth; I knew that I had finally started to live.

I returned to covering the wars. It's steady work. And I know how to do it. Now every time some young reporter writes a beautifully crafted piece about a promising cease-fire or a new peace deal, I think of Brando: "The warrior will always triumph over the poet."

That's the flawed evolution we've been handed. In some other corner of the universe, the laws of existence must be reversed. Surely, not every manifestation of life is this fucked up. Somewhere, the long victory ends up going to the plodding, pacific parasite who lives outside history and its multitude of mad scribes.

But not here. That's not our story. Here, the warrior always triumphs over the poet. The only mistake I made was insisting all along that the warrior had been Brando.

My flight to Delhi was delayed. No fault of Schiphol's: the plane hadn't arrived from India. I waited in a chair far from the gate. The other travelers were tired also. Some slumped in their seats. The sleek chairs were engineered to be just comfortable enough, but not so much so that you could forget you were just passing through. A couple spoke in soft whispers to each other—a honeymoon. Across from them, a man sat alone with his briefcase on his lap. A skinny boy broke free from his mother and ran across the terminal. He was laughing, delighting in his freedom. But something in his slender limbs took me back, and suddenly I recalled the war orphan in Kandahar. His small arm waving good-bye, the yawning Afghan desert before me. Thank you, Mrs. Mister.

I've learned that it's hard to hide in the middle of a journey. People reveal themselves. If you make a living from watching them, you understand what they're saying. Everyone has their own way of moving, of touching, of turning away. A hand on a hip, a scowl, a closing and shutting of the eyes. I picked out the vacationing Americans, the wounded soldier, the new parents. Very close to the gate, a woman sat alone. She was slim, dressed in black. A book was open on her lap, and she was surrounded by bags and packages. Her face was drawn, and her arms were crossed over her chest. She met my eyes, and I looked away.

Across the corridor, an old man with a limp cleaned the darkening windows. The attendants made an announcement that I didn't understand. After a while, I closed my eyes and slept.

Sometime in the night I woke, a chill and sudden dread. A sense of falling. But it passed quickly. A few minutes later, my flight was called, and after a moment's hesitation, I rose to stand in line with everyone else.

Acknowledgments

Many thanks to my agent, Joy Harris, who patiently read multiple versions of this story and whose calm guidance made all the difference. Thank you also to my equally patient and talented editor, Gillian Blake. I'm especially indebted to my loyal sister, Rosa Menéndez, and my dear friend Diana Abu-Jaber, who read, listened, and carried me through the many manifestations of this story, both the real and the imagined. Thanks also to the wise advice of Ileana Oroza, John Lantigua, Junot Díaz, Margaria Fichtner, Jenny Krugman, Sheppard Speer, Alan Cheuse, and, as ever, Breyten Breytenbach. The *Miami Herald* photographer Charles Trainor Jr. gave me invaluable insight into the work of a photojournalist and saved me from embarrassing errors, and Carl Juste lent his art and optimism. I am grateful also for all I learned from Michael Adams and my students and colleagues at UT Austin. In Istanbul, Şenel Yavaser and Şebnem Arsu introduced me to one of the world's great cities. I shall never forget them or their friendship.

And to Dexter Filkins, who showed me the whole world, my everlasting gratitude and affection.

About the author

2 Last Meals

About the book

5 The Exile and the Nomad Are
Cousins: An Interview with
Ana Menéndez

Read on

11 An Archeological Record of
The Last War

Insights,
Interviews
& More...

Last Meals

I SHOPPED FOR THE FISH that morning, waking early to make the fifteen-minute walk from my apartment to Balık Pazarı before the day's stock ran out. One kilo of *levrek* (Turkish for a kind of sea bass) and then some lettuce and tomatoes from the guy who always slipped in something extra. I took my time walking back along Istanbul's glorious Independence Street, stopping along the way to buy some butter cookies. For dessert, I would make individual cheesecake tarts. I spent the rest of the day cooking a "welcome home" meal for my husband, who was returning from a reporting tour in Baghdad. Pan-fried *levrek*, fresh bread, and a big green salad, the entire meal an act of love and dedication that belied the fact that my marriage was ending.

It has always been like this. I could mark the milestones in my life by what I was cooking and eating at the time: the subdued Christmas Eve dinner of roast pork and rice and beans we shared as a family a week before my aunt's death, the white bean stews my Asturian grandfather made when my mother was pregnant with my sister, the smell of fried onions and potatoes that still reminds me of my grandmother's house.

The happiest memories of my marriage were anchored by food: the fish soup my husband and I shared in the Cinque Terre on our first trip abroad, the chocolate croissant he bought for me in

> ❝ I could mark the milestones in my life by what I was cooking and eating at the time. ❞

Sancerre when I was exhausted from the last leg of a long bike trip, the lamb tagine we cooked together when we were training for a marathon in Miami. I was with him when I tasted my first pomegranate on a reporting trip in Afghanistan and when I had my first piece of yak meat in Bhutan. Our life together was defined by writing, food, and travel, and so was the end of that life.

My sister was with me the day I served my husband with divorce papers. I turned the ringer off on my phone, thawed two pounds of frozen scallops, cooked them in a ridiculous amount of butter, sprinkled them with red pepper flakes, and served them alongside a bottle of Spanish Cava. It was delicious.

For years, Americans have had a strained relationship with food. Eating and dining have become the expression of a collective neurosis: food as status symbol, the ultimate fashion accessory. Meals that should have nourished have become instead a repository for our misplaced fears and manias. Perhaps the new economy will return dining, however temporarily, to what it was for most of human history and continues to be in much of the world: a communal expression of joy, the creative intersection of basic sustenance and magic art.

When I talk to students about writing, I often invoke the metaphor of cooking. Like cooking, writing is about transformation—it's about ▶

> **"** Our life together was defined by writing, food, and travel, and so was the end of that life. **"**

taking the raw, indigestible experience of life and creating something entirely new, something sustaining, something shared. I especially like the metaphor because so much of what women write is belittled as "kitchen-sink drama." But truth is revealed in the small details of our stories, in the individual lives of ordinary people struggling through loss and sorrow.

During those long hard months when my marriage was ending, cooking kept me alive. I worked at home, which gave me the luxury of being able to prepare three hot meals a day, usually some variation of oatmeal, grilled fish, and homemade chili. On the wall separating my kitchen from my dining room, I wrote, in three-inch letters, the defiant words of the eighteenth-century clergyman Sydney Smith: "Fate cannot harm me—I have dined today."

I dined and dined, and Fate kept a gentle distance. I cooked dozens of meals in my tiny kitchen, most of them shared with friends and family. And day by day the sad memories were transformed into the kind of melancholy lessons that help us grow wise and strong.

Food is not the answer to heartbreak. But in the slow patient alchemy that is cooking, we might find a measure of solace, and a reminder that time and imagination can sometimes make tender the toughest sorrow. ∽

66 Writing is about . . . taking the raw, indigestible experience of life and creating something entirely new, something sustaining, something shared. 99

The Exile and the Nomad Are Cousins
An Interview with Ana Menéndez

by Amy Letter

Originally published by *The Rumpus*: www.therumpus.net.

The Rumpus: I'd like to make my first question "the obvious one": since the novel is in part based on some of your own experiences, how much are you willing to share about the experiences that inspired this novel? Can you give us the backstory of the authority with which you write?

Ana Menéndez: All writing—all art, really—is personal; the rest is abstraction. In some works, I think, the direct experience is, shall we say, less filtered. I began this novel in 2003, as I was finishing *Loving Che*. It was supposed to be about a man, Alexander, who arrives in Istanbul with a past— in Afghanistan he was responsible for a boy's death. He works out his demons amid the ruin and multilayered splendor of Istanbul. I was almost midway through the writing when, in June 2004, I received an anonymous letter alleging that my husband was cheating on me in Baghdad, where he was working as a correspondent for the *New York Times*. ▶

> 66 All writing— all art, really—is personal; the rest is abstraction. In some works, I think, the direct experience is, shall we say, less filtered. 99

The Exile and the Nomad Are Cousins
(*continued*)

Among the many disruptions the letter caused, not least was a blow to my writing. I found that I simply couldn't create any more. I eventually moved to Miami, filed for divorce, and started working as a columnist for the *Miami Herald*. But still I could not finish the novel. One night, in frustration and just wanting to write, I began to put down the story of the letter. I didn't intend to publish it. But, in the mysterious alchemy of writing, the fiction story and the real story merged. Characters hopped the fictional divide. A new story emerged that was beyond anything I could put down. I don't know where it came from, but I was happy to be writing again.

There is much that is pure invention in *The Last War* and much that draws on real experience. I did travel the war zones with my husband (though not to the extent Flash did) and I did receive a letter. But because Flash is not me, I was able to see her predicament quite coolly. She is a photographer who has made a life from peering into other people's suffering. Her camera reveals subtle insights. But she's never—until perhaps the very end—able to turn that probing lens onto herself.

Rumpus: Did your original character, Alexander, morph into Alexandra, the

66 In the mysterious alchemy of writing, the fiction story and the real story merged. Characters hopped the fictional divide. 99

6

character that seems to haunt Flash in *The Last War*? If so, was that a difficult process?

Menéndez: Yes, Alexander morphed into Alexandra. He did it all by himself, with little help from me. The writing just took on its own logic. In the first rendering, there was a strong narrator "I" telling Alexander's story, so everything just shifted naturally.

Rumpus: Let's talk about the ending a little bit. Your novel's long epilogue was, I think, a daring choice. I spent days trying to reconcile the story I thought I knew with the epilogue.

Menéndez: I knew from the start I would have to include one, mainly to show that Flash learns a little but it's not enough to make her change. She is basically the same person she was at the beginning. The epilogue also gives Alexandra a chance to express a small kindness—in her insistence that Brando had been faithful. Whether the reader believes it or not, Flash seems to buy it.

Rumpus: The idea that Brando/Wonderboy had been faithful seems to me to recharacterize Alexandra as far more vindictive. Can you give us more insight into this character? ▸

> " Flash learns a little but it's not enough to make her change. "

The Exile and the Nomad Are Cousins
(continued)

Menéndez: I hope that the insight develops out of the reading, and I'd rather leave it to each reader to draw his or her own. Some people have said that at the end she seems even more cruel than ever, and others see someone (an earth mother, perhaps) who is trying to soothe Flash and bring her peace, however much of a lie it is.

Rumpus: How do you feel about the immediate connection many readers will make between love and war (or marriage and war, etc.)?

Menéndez: It's a classic connection and a natural one. Both represent the more intense extremes humans are capable of. I explored this idea a little in *Loving Che* as well: the intensity of love is very much like the destabilizing, greater-than-oneself high that human beings also experience in war and strife. It's one of the reasons I think we will never be able to banish war. No one wants to admit it, but war offers a transforming experience that taps right into the addictive pleasure of power and destruction.

Rumpus: Your previous books have been about exiles. How do you see the exile experience playing into this book? Are you familiar with Ovid's exile on the Black Sea, and if so, did that play into

66 The intensity of love is very much like the destabilizing, greater-than-oneself high that human beings also experience in war and strife. It's one of the reasons I think we will never be able to banish war. 99

your thoughts at all when you were writing this novel?

Menéndez: Exile is very much a part of this book, and Ovid and his *Tristia* very much haunt the shadows of *The Last War*. I reread a lot of the *Metamorphoses* during the time I was writing and also the new translations (by multiple poets) of the Odes of Horace. There is nothing more refreshing, humbling, and ultimately inspiring for a writer than the classics. Even when we're not aware of it, they permeate what we write and what we believe. Even Minerva (whose name has its roots in "memory") lurks in the shadows of this book. None of this is too overt in the writing itself (at least I hope it's not). Instead, these very ancient themes form a distant backdrop for the book because they inform my own life (all our lives, really).

Like love and war, the theme of exile is a very classic one (*The Odyssey* of course being the most obvious example), and I've always been interested in it for obvious reasons. As a little girl, I was fascinated by this mystical place, this Eden, that my parents had been banished from. The children of exiles grow up with a kind of void at their back. In time, at least in me, this void (this unknowable world) transformed itself from a physical displacement to a metaphorical, or ▶

> **❝** There is nothing more refreshing, humbling, and ultimately inspiring for a writer than the classics. Even when we're not aware of it, they permeate what we write and what we believe. **❞**

9

The Exile and the Nomad Are Cousins
(continued)

spiritual, displacement—a
disconnection from clan and tribe
that perhaps inspired me to wander
the world (the exile and nomad are
cousins, after all). But I'm also curious
about how we are exiles from ourselves,
how ultimately the individual human
experience is a lonely one. ∽

An Archeological Record of *The Last War*

EVERY NOVEL is something of an archeological record—of the general time in which it was written as well as of all the flotsam and jetsam that washed up on the shore of the author's imagination. Most people who write come to the task through reading. Inevitably, all that reading leaves an impression. I was an undergraduate the first time I read Dostoevsky's novella *The Eternal Husband*. But it wasn't until I encountered it again some years later that the force of its ideas and characters really hit me. Here was a glib, destructive character who seemed to have no sense of the effect of his actions and, perhaps as a consequence, lacked the ability to change. Alexei Ivanovich Velchaninov continued to fascinate me throughout my graduate studies when the mantra of the workshop was "the character must change!" But what about a character so self-deluded that change is not possible? When I was creating Flash, this was the model I kept coming back to. But such a character requires some kind of conscience, even if it resides in another person. And so Alexandra appeared on the scene. The name Truso is a humble nod to the master who created Alexei Ivanovich Velchaninov and Pavel Pavlovich Trusotsky and set them at odds under a midnight sun.

Here are some other books that ▶

> ❝ Every novel is something of an archeological record—of the general time in which it was written as well as of all the flotsam and jetsam that washed up on the shore of the author's imagination. ❞

An Archeological Record of *The Last War*
(continued)

influenced or inspired me as I was
writing:

- *The Light Garden of the Angel King:
  Travels in Afghanistan with Bruce
  Chatwin,* by Peter Levi
- *The Great Game: The Struggle
  for Empire in Central Asia,*
  by Peter Hopkirk
- *Seeing Through Places: Reflections
  on Geography and Identity,*
  by Mary Gordon
- *The Narrow Road to the Deep
  North and Other Travel Sketches,*
  by Matsuo Basho; Nobuyuki Yuasa,
  translator
- *On Photography,* by Susan Sontag
- *Istanbul,* by Orhan Pamuk
- *The Emigrants,* by W. G. Sebald

Don't miss the next
book by your favorite
author. Sign up now for
AuthorTracker by visiting
www.AuthorTracker.com.